TOMORROW, MAYBE

GO THERE.

OTHER TITLES AVAILABLE FROM PUSH

Cut
PATRICIA McCORMICK

Fighting Ruben Wolfe
MARCUS ZUSAK

I Will Survive
KRISTEN KEMP

Kerosene
CHRIS WOODING

Nowhere Fast
KEVIN WALTMAN

Pure Sunshine
BRIAN JAMES

You Are Here, This Is Now:
The Best Young Writers and Artists in America
EDITED BY DAVID LEVITHAN

You Remind Me of You
EIREANN CORRIGAN

TOMORROW, MAYBE

BRIAN JAMES

SCHOLASTIC INC.

NEW YORK TORONTO LONDON AUCKLAND SYDNEY

MEXICO CITY NEW DELHI HONG KONG BUENOS AIRES

ISBN 0-439-49035-9

Copyright © 2003 by Brian James.

All rights reserved. Published by PUSH, an imprint of Scholastic Inc., 557 Broadway, New York, NY 10012.

SCHOLASTIC and associated logos are trademarks and/or registered trademarks of Scholastic Inc.

12 11 10 9 8 7 6 5 4 3 2 1   3 4 5 6 7 8/0

Printed in the U.S.A.   40
First Scholastic/PUSH printing, March 2003

for all the lost kids

–If you let yourself go and opened your mind
I'll bet you'd be doing like me
And it so bad–
–Layne Staley

ACKNOWLEDGMENTS

Sarah – For putting up with me through anything and still always smiling. I love you all up.

Christian – See you in Vegas!

Doggie – For being my faithful cat.

Richard Brautigan – Be forever in watermelon sugar.

Frances Bean Cobain – "leave a blanket of ash on the ground."

My Family – See you at Thanksgiving!

David (of course) – Thanks for everything.

Joan M – whose letter from Brown County Jail School was lost on a Continental flight from NYC to Seattle before I had the chance to answer it. I'm sorry, and thank you!

While I look around, I wonder how these became the people in my life. How did I get here? Who are we? Who am I? While I sit here, I wonder. This is not what the tv promised. This isn't my dream. I never wanted to end up this way, but that's what happens, I guess. They don't tell you that in the commercials. They don't tell you this when you visit the doctor, or when you are in grade school and write "What I want to be when I grow up" essays. I never said I wanted to be homeless. I never said I wanted to end up like this. I never fucking wanted any of this.

It's cold in here. We're all huddled together. have to keep warm. It's disgusting. curled up together like dirty rats. It's so ugly. We're so ugly. this place. this place is all we have, all we have to call home. Smells like piss in here. The boy leaning against me smells like piss and I'm not even sure what his name is.

Just a place to spend the night. to get out of the cold and off the streets. Pretty much like every night. Nothing changes. This town never changes. The people never change. It's always the same kids everywhere I seem to go. That's the only thing that makes us stick together. habit maybe. maybe we really do like each other maybe. Or maybe it's just because we always seem to find ourselves in the same places, at the same time, with the same needs and nowhere else to go.

It's okay really. It's not that bad, really. I mean, I don't want anyone feeling sorry for me or anything. It's no one's fault. Doesn't really bother me. It's just that for once, I wish I knew the people who were sleeping around me. really knew them. where they came from. where they want to go. their favorite cereal. favorite color. any of those things that matter when you're a streetkid. But it's a rule. No one tells their story. No one wants to hear another sad tale. Your own is sad enough. no more sympathy left over for anyone else but yourself. But just once, I wish I could. feel sorry for someone else, I mean.

I love when the sky is gray. when the dawn paints the roofs of the buildings and the sun is still hiding. The city is ours then. Right before everyone takes over, right when everyone is still sleeping. It's hard to notice that it's so cold when it's this pretty.

It's like that today. I made Jef come out here with me. Sure, he complained. He didn't want to wake up, but I can always get him to come along. *–Please! Please!–* that's all I have to say. He likes me. sees me as his little sister or something. I don't mind. It's nice actually.

He's kind of grumpy today, though. He doesn't see things like I do. didn't sleep well last night. He's kind of pissed I woke him up but if I keep smiling at him and at the sky, the trees, the pigeons, then eventually he'll come around.

–Chan, why do you always drag me here? I hate fucking Tompkins Square!–

3

My name's really Gretchen, but they all started calling me Chan. At least Jef did and everyone else seemed to adopt it. like a pet name. I like that. Chan. It means "little girl" in Japan.

He's rubbing his hands together. His fingernails are dirty. so is his hair. But his eyes are clean. his voice is clean. Dirty on the outside. that's alright. It's only if you let it sink in. He sips the coffee we stole from the deli. sips it twice before he looks over at me again.

–*Because. It's beautiful here!*– I tell him. Then I smile again and finally, FINALLY, he smiles back.

–*Beautiful, huh? I guess if you think garbage and dog shit's beautiful.*– I punch him in the arm for making fun of me. I know he's only kidding. Still, he's sort of a jerk. I'm glad when he spills his coffee a little.

Jef tries to warm up to me. Says he's sorry and all that. making puppy faces and everything. But I don't care.

I'm mad. I don't care that the sky is gray. It was so pretty and he ruined it. He shouldn't kid about things. about the morning sky when you're seeing the trees in the park. the birds. and all the pain goes away and the traffic is dead on

4

the streets. It's the only time I really feel that I know who I am.

We sit there awhile. Quiet. I'm not speaking to him. I'm sad now. sad for no reason and that makes me angry. I'm angry and that makes me sadder and I blame Jef for everything. I know he thinks I'm being childish, and that makes me angrier. Why did he have to ruin the whole day?

–*C'mon, let's get something to eat. C'mon, I'm sorry, okay? See? I'm looking up at the sky. You're right. It is pretty. Can we go get something to eat now?*–

–*Yeah we can. Asshole!*– because it isn't pretty anymore. It's crowded. The people have all woken up. have come out with their clean clothes and their new day smells. It's only happy when it's lonely. –*And you're paying!*–

Jef's way ahead, walking really fast. I keep back a little bit. keep it slow. walking with my head down to let him know I haven't forgiven him. not 100% anyway. to let him know I'm not going to be running around all day just because he's all racy and everything. Not my problem.

*   *   *

5

I'm out of breath. I want to stop running. I don't care if they catch me. I did nothing wrong. So what? I was hungry. They gonna shoot me for that? Let them. I just want to catch my breath. Jef keeps pulling me by the hand. Every time I slow down, he pulls harder. almost rips my arm right off from my shoulder. He doesn't want to stop. doesn't want to be caught again. I think he's carrying. He doesn't want to spend another night in jail. So we run.

I knew he didn't have money on him when we went in there. I knew! –*Don't worry*– he said. –*I made some cash last night*– he said.

I see myself in the reflection bouncing off the store windows. skinny. dirty. walking dead. I hate seeing myself. Especially when I'm running down the sidewalk like a criminal. I hate seeing myself like that. like who I am.

They'll give up after a few more blocks. That's how the police are. We're only worth four, five blocks at the most. Then I can rest. I have to keep running until then. I'm out of breath so it's hard but I keep going.

I'm right, though. Once we turn the last corner, I don't hear their heavy footsteps anymore. don't hear the mean voice. the sight of his badge like he thinks it means something to us. I only hear the sound of my own breath. the sound of Jef breathing like he is going to explode. We keep running for three more blocks just to be safe. keep running until we're somewhere we know we can hide.

We will always get away. always, because we'll always be together. Those heavy footsteps. cop steps. they'll always be behind us. always be too slow. because nothing can ever happen to me. nothing worse than anything else. nothing that I can't handle because I'm never alone out here. on the streets. Never.

The building is right there. The place where we live because no one else wants to. No one else wants to live in such a run-down building so that's why it's empty. that's why we move in like shadows. We fill in the background of everything in this city. We fill in the empty spaces.

We enter the building from the back, through the vacant lot. another squat. It's one we haven't stayed in lately, but one where we know some kids anyway. We'll be okay hanging out here. I can hear voices on the second floor. It's dark but we find the stairs. You just kind of naturally know your way around. You get a feeling for these things. Minor details differ, that's all.

There's two people sleeping at the top of the stairs. a guy and a girl. Scott and Lily. Both of them are so skinny they've almost become invisible. Skeletons only. The bones in their faces are swollen. It makes them look like each other. I've known them since I came to the city. They've always been together. belong together because they look like each other. The same dirty brown hair. the same number of ribs showing through their skin. I think it's sweet. Jef says they're only together because they get high together. I think it's more than that, though. I think they love each other.

We step over Scott. He doesn't move but Lily yells at us without looking. She's pissed we disturbed them, but I'm not sure she even really woke up. We go into the next room where the voices were coming from. I see three faces. Shadows anyway. I don't recognize them but Jef whispers that it's okay. He knows them so we go in.

–Jef the Meth, what a surprise!– one of the guys says. He seems happy enough to see us. doesn't look dangerous at least. *–What brings you to our lovely, lively establishment?–*

–Nothing much. How's it going?– and Jef shakes hands with him. *–Ty, this is Chan. Chan, Ty. We were looking to crash here for a bit. Skipped out on a breakfast tab and the fuzz were chasing us, you know how it is.–*

–I certainly do– he says with a smile. crooked teeth smile. rubs his goatee. red devil goatee where his hair is red like natural strawberries. Sounds creepy, but he's not. He's almost dashing. like a knight or something. like something from an old story. *–Well, that's okay with us, ain't it fellas? Never one to begrudge a man in need. Or a pretty young lady at that.–*

I thank him. I kind of smile at him. Not too much though. He's older than me. maybe 20's. They all are. older than me, I mean. Not as much as him, as Ty. a year or two maybe. But he's more than that. 5 or 6 years. I'm only 15. I'm the youngest one in the room by far. That makes me nervous. It's not safe being the youngest. I know it's only because the police were chasing us. I'm still a little paranoid. Nothing's going to happen. In a few minutes it will pass. I will feel safe again. always only takes a few minutes. I hate feeling scared.

I learn the names of the other two guys. Eric is one. He came here from L.A. a few months ago. thought it would be easier. He seems nice enough. I could get to like him, I guess. His soft eyes give him that look. like he's sensitive, you know. California eyes. a faint tan covering his skin still, but almost gone here in the winter. and the small tattoo. on his forearm. I think it's a butterfly until I get a close look. It's a dragon. It looks a little silly. Doesn't match him, really. his soft eyes. It's supposed to look mean, but it looks friendly.

Marc is the other one. He definitely scares me. It's not because he's black, so don't go thinking that about me. I'm not like that. you can't afford to be if you live on the streets. It's something else. something about his eyes. They're red. or reddish anyway. I will never trust anyone with eyes like that.

They're all sipping it. the alcohol. just little sips. to keep warm. I don't like it. the way it tastes. But it's cold. so I take a sip. Ty tells me it's okay. I don't even know him and I'm not sure I want him telling me what's okay and what isn't. but he's alright, really. I don't mean to be mean. really, he's nice. I'm just nervous. I'm always nervous. I hate it. So I try to be especially nice to him. He probably didn't even think I was being mean or anything but I felt bad.

He's lived so many places. He tells me about them as the bottle passes around from one mouth to the next. –*You look like a girl I knew in Berlin. Same eyes. You ever been to Berlin?–*

–No.– I've never been anywhere. nowhere exotic like how I'm picturing Berlin when he says it. The way he says it. picturing electric lights like slot machines in Atlantic City because I was there once a long time ago. –*Is that where you're from?–* I ask quietly. dreamingly.

He laughs. says –*no.–* says –*nah, I'm from Pittsburgh. I've just been around a lot. You know, need to experience my fellow man and all that crap.–* and he rubs his electric red goatee like someone who is much wiser than I am.

And I want him to tell me about everyplace he's ever been. about the time he went backpacking over Europe and that's how he ended up in Berlin. about how he was in the desert in Mexico and learned to shoot a gun at green colored bottles and green colored lizards. And he tells me all about it. about everything and I sit listening like storytime. like I could just sit here listening to him all day and all night.

–*So?–* I start to ask him then shake my head because I know I shouldn't. know I should never ask anyone this question. But I want to know, so I ask anyway. –*So, how did you end up here? On the streets, I mean.–*

–I want to be here– he says and I think that's totally crazy. *–Here's freedom, man! Here is where you can be anything. This is home.–* and it sounds so pretty put that way. sounds so pretty I almost want to believe it.

When the bottle comes around again, Jef passes it the other way. he doesn't want me to have any. I don't want any more anyway. but he likes to think he's looking out for me. I let him think that. it makes him happy.

I'm tired. I lie down next to Jef. He puts his arm around me. my eyes barely open. It feels nice to have someone care about you once in a while. I close my eyes. I feel like I'm floating. like a dancer or a cloud or something. It's not until then that I notice I'm no longer nervous. I'm drifting off to sleep and I think maybe I'm happy. at least for right now anyway and that's all that counts.

I dream I'm a little girl again, lying in the back of my dad's pickup truck staring at the sky. It's twilight. The trees are screaming by a thousand miles per hour. the telephone poles too. the electric lines. the birds. Nothing can touch me when I'm there. I'm not connected to my body then. I'm flying like the birds.

It's not what you think. me being on the streets and everything. My dad didn't abuse me or anything like that. He was okay actually. But he loved my stepmom too much. She was a bitch. I don't think she liked me much. not that I made it easy for her. In fact, I hated her from the start. She was a tramp. not right for my dad. She just moved right in after my mom died. It was hard for me. I was lonely. I thought I could make it go away if I just got away.

My stepmom smoked a lot. always smelled like menthol. always told me I wasn't any good. wasn't smart enough. wasn't pretty enough. *—You'll end up a no good whore like your mama—* OR LIKE YOU! that's what I should've said. I never did. too afraid I guess.

She was plain mean. never let me do anything. never let me go anywhere or see anyone. never let me leave the house. like a prisoner. One time, I wanted to go to this party. It was stupid really. just a stupid party with balloons and spin-the-bottle and stuff. But I really wanted to go.

I remember everything about it. about getting ready for it. how there was this boy I really liked who was going. this boy who was going to be my boyfriend at the party because that's how boys and girls work when you're 11. So I put on this tank top. purple. It had sparkles on it and a star printed on the front. And I put on lipstick. pink lipstick. I felt so smart. so mature, I guess. That didn't last. didn't last even 10 minutes because my stepmom came into my room. She didn't knock or anything. She came in and stood in the doorway. A cigarette burning in her ugly hands. The smell of alcohol on her ugly breath. She stood there, watching me watch myself in the mirror. She laughed at me. I mean, really laughed *at* me. *–Oh, don't you look stupid–* she said.

I pretended it didn't hurt. pretended there weren't any tears in my eyes even though she could see them. Pretended and told her I didn't care what she thought. told her how everyone was going to say I looked great. *–I don't think so, because I don't think you're going–* she said. Then she dropped the cigarette on the carpet. Burning black hole and she stamped it out. *—I don't think you're going until this stain comes out—* and she shut the door. shutting me in the whole night.

I couldn't breathe around her. was so trapped there. always jealous of the birds that way. how they can fly I mean. how free they are. I wanted that. wanted to get away. wanted a new life with new people. so I ran away.

I was 13. I couldn't go back if I wanted to. I don't want to. But it's nice to go back there in my dreams. Things are always better when you're only remembering them.

Sure, there's things I miss. I miss having a room. miss my stuff. my dolls. I miss this old notebook that I kept a diary in when I was 10 for about 2 days. I miss the sound our microwave made when it was done. Or the way the remote for the tv was missing the back and the batteries were always falling out whenever I put it down. I miss my dad a little too. He probably misses me. It's pretty to think so anyway. I miss school, but not that much. Never really had many friends. everyone there was pretty well-off. I do miss having a place to go every day. the routine. waiting for the bus, waiting for it to pick me up. waiting at the end of the day for it to take me home. I miss all of that, but I find ways. I enjoy my freedom just as much as I would probably enjoy the things I miss. So one way or the other, I guess it doesn't really matter. I'll get by.

It's dark when I open my eyes. another day gone. the guys are all sleeping. They look so cute. like little babies almost. It makes me smile.

My legs are cramped. I need to walk around and stretch them out. Scott and Lily are still pretty much dead. Their faces pressed together like identical twins. Their eyes closed so you can't see that maybe the color is different. And when they breathe, they breathe together, silently. It's the perfect time to make my way onto the roof. I watch the city light up. It's almost as nice as in the morning. electricity switching on in every building.

I never saw tall buildings growing up. It's pretty rural where my dad lives. So I'm still fascinated by the skyscrapers. I don't think I'll ever get used to them. The kids who grew up here tease me about it, say I'm so suburban and all that but it doesn't bother me. I just feel bad for them. They take too much for granted.

It's really cold up on the roof. the wind's always stronger. I wrap my coat tighter around me. It's not much of a coat.

Doesn't help that I only have a t-shirt on under it either. but that's all I'll wear. My shirt is my favorite thing I own. the only thing I own, really. it's nothing fancy. plain white. it's got a smiling daisy on it. it's not much. but somehow, it makes me happy. makes everyone happy to see me too. that's why I wear it. even when it's cold like it is today.

It almost smells like it's going to snow. I hope it does. Someone will throw a party if it does. we always do. kind of a tradition. that would be fun. but for now, I'll just enjoy the scenery even if it doesn't snow.

I haven't been able to decide which I like better. which of the buildings, I mean. They're all so tall, so perfect. the way they seem to lean on each other. Sometimes I think I like the Empire State Building most of all. The way the lights change with the seasons. the way it stands so much taller than the rest. But then I see the other buildings. the nameless ones and I think that makes them more special. I can't choose. I go back and forth. sometimes this one. sometimes that one. I figure I'll never come to a conclusion, which sucks because I have to keep turning my head to look at all of them. I like to pretend there are angels jumping from one to the top of the other. Only I can see them. can watch them play. That way I don't miss the stars. You can't see the stars from the city. not unless it's really

17

cold. colder than it is today. When it's that cold I don't like watching the city. I like to be inside then. I like to be warm.

Jef's awake when I go back downstairs. at least he wakes up when I come in anyway. *—Where did you go?—* he asks. It's almost a whisper. He doesn't want to wake up anyone else.

—I was upstairs. On the roof— I say.

—Same old Chan.— He smiles at me. He lifts his arm up for me to curl up next to him again. It feels safe there. snuggled up against him. falling back asleep again. slowly.

Everyone is talking really loud. really fast too. I wake up. Sitting up, I rub my eyes. Scott and Lily are in the room. Awake finally. They say hello to me and I wave back. I'm not good at waking up. I'm cranky and they are moving so fast. I feel really slow.

–*C'mon guys let's get the fuck out of here! I wanna fucking party!*– Lily is dancing around the room. She is the only one who hears any music. No one is paying any attention to her. It's how she always is. like a firecracker or something else that's ready to snap, leaving powder everywhere. She's just restless. It happens when you stay inside all day. She just wants everyone to look at her. at the way she moves. her bones twisting together like some beautiful alien.

–*Where the hell we gonna go? Just sit down. Please!*– Scott says, grabbing Lily and pulling her down. Everyone laughs, including Lily. –*You're making me nervous running around like a monkey and all.*–

Lily sits. frowns. the ceiling frowns with her. all the holes in the wall. like faces. they frown too.

It's funny how the house is like us. most of the walls hollowed out so only the beams show like ribs in a skeleton. thin like we are. all the windows shut up with boards like streetkids with their eyes closed on the sidewalk. No wallpaper or nice clothing. all drab colors. No decorations to lighten up the mood and I reach for the spot on my neck where I once had a silver chain but don't anymore.

When I was little, I would have thought this was a haunted house. the broken floorboards and cobwebs. but it's not spooky now. now that I'm used to filth.

Ty is trying to start a fire out of some pieces of the wall. It doesn't look that safe, but we're really cold. Besides, it doesn't look as if he'll ever get it going. No one stops him.

I lean on Jef and put my head back. I can feel his voice where my ear is pushed against his chest. *–How long you been here? You're gonna like it. it's not warm like California or nothing, but it's way fucking cooler.–* He's talking to Eric. speaking fast. I think he wants Eric to feel at home.

20

–Oh, you been?– Eric asks. his tan face glows in the darkness.

–Been where?–

–California.–

–Never!– Jef says. *–there's no need if you're in New York, that's what I'm saying to you.–* Eric smiles politely. *–everything here's for the taking!–*

I remember him giving me the same talk when I came. how scared I was to say anything. kind of like Eric now. Jef giving his speech about free things to be found at every turn. I remember all I could think was Templeton the Rat. from *Charlotte's Web*. Jef's ears getting all red when he's excited.

I laugh at the memory.

–I'll show you what I mean. tomorrow. me and you– he says and makes Eric shake on it. Jef's talking works on Eric like it worked on me. making him feel welcome.

I try not to listen. try to give them some privacy. Marc has moved up next to me. it kinda skeeves me out. He's

21

RIGHT next to me! trying to touch my hand and all. –*Hey, hey? wanna play patty-cake, baby?*– Christ! He's so gross. those red eyes staring at me. I wish he'd just leave me alone! I don't know who he thinks I am. We're not all like that. girls, I mean. I keep pushing him away. I'm nice about it, don't get me wrong. I don't want to be rude. This is not our place. mine and Jef's. We're just guests here.

–*You know, we got to be nice to each other out here. love one another, you know. love your brother.*– and he laughs because he thinks that's clever.

–*Yeah, but you're a creep*– I say. pretend to be joking and he believes that I am, so he keeps talking. Great! Should have just been serious.

–*Yeah, it's like this. regular people don't understand us. they're all about money and status. the lexus and what have you. not us. we're about love and all that. me and you. that's us.*–

Us? what is he thinking? that I'm 15 so therefore I'm going to believe his bullshit. You don't understand me! I want to say. I'm not as sweet as you think I am. I'm much more. But he'll never know because he keeps talking. I keep listening. pretending to be interested. nodding. looking sweet and innocent. That's my specialty. how I get by. It's disgusting how bad he's trying to impress me. trying to hit on me. it grosses me out.

The conversation stops when she comes to the top of the steps. Everyone turns to stare at her. She looks so small. so frightened. The messy strands of black hair in front of her eyes are like midnight. Tangled like an old doll's. Her eyes. so clear and so blue. Her eyes shining like twinkling stars behind her hair. Her hair like midnight, and her hand shakes. shakes because it's cold. because her whole body is shaking. Her hand is so small I think I could fit it completely in my palm. so small as she holds it up to her face. trembling like her lower lip is trembling.

She doesn't move when she sees us. just stands there. like a rabbit when cars cross their path on the highway. I can't take my eyes off her. I think she must be lost. I think her parents must be outside on the street frantically asking everyone if they've seen their daughter because they got separated on the busy sidewalks. I think that because there's no way she's here on purpose. No way she ran away. No way because she's too small for that to have happened.

–Get the fuck out of here! I told you last time, you can't stay here!–

I look at Ty when he yells at her. I don't understand why he's so mad. It's a little kid. He throws a piece of plaster at her. She doesn't move.

–What's the matter with you?– I scream.

I don't know why I say it. Everyone looks at me funny. like I'm the one who's crazy. But I'm not the one! she's a little kid!

Ty's pretty stunned. I'm standing up. yelling at him. Jef is a little shocked too. surprised by how mad I seem. I'm also a little surprised to tell the truth. not sure what is coming over me. maybe it is partly because I just woke up. maybe I'm angry that they are all ignoring her. maybe it's just the way the girl looks. So afraid.

–What's with you?– Ty says, rubbing his chin like it is on fire. The hair like fire and it looks mean now. Not like earlier.

–What's with me?– and I can't keep my voice steady. *–What's the matter with you! Throwing things at her. She's just a little kid!–*

24

–Yeah, an annoying little kid. The fucking brat has come around here every day for the last week.– Ty's getting a little mad at me. He knows what I'm going to say. Knows what I want without me saying it so he says it first. *–She can't fucking stay. I'm not a babysitter. She's bad news all the way. A kid like that will bring the police around. Hell, you being here's bad enough. A kid like her would bring the police around.–*

–SO you're just going to let her freeze to death.–

–Fine, you want to take care of her? Be my guest. Go ahead. But if she brings any heat on us, I'm leaving you both right where I found you.–

I look at Jef. He shrugs his shoulders, which means I can do whatever I want. he doesn't care. no one does. Eric's laughing even, saying *–That girl's tough, huh? Good for you.–* Ty smiles. I don't think he's mad really. I am, though. asshole.

The girl still hasn't moved from the top of the stairs. she is surprised. I don't think she expected to stay. Apparently this is her fifth time coming here. stubborn little thing, have to give her that. I walk over to her. Everyone else goes back to whatever it is they were doing.

She backs away a little. then stays. she lets me get close. I hold her hands in mine. They fit perfectly. They fit and they are so cold. so red. I try to warm them the best I can. I smile at her. She doesn't smile back. I don't blame her. I was the same way my first time.

She doesn't want to go over by the fire that Ty got going. that's understandable. I mean some scary guy just threw a piece of the wall at her. I want to go over there but I don't. I sit down with the girl. We use Scott's blanket. It is warm enough, I suppose. comfortable anyway.

She doesn't want to talk so I do all the talking. I tell her who everyone is. Pointing them out and watching her small eyes dart back and forth at each one. darting back and forth from them to the stairs like she's keeping lookout just in case she needs to run away in a hurry. I tell her that they aren't so bad once you get to know them.

–*What's your name?*– I ask, still holding her hands in mine. Breathing on them and slowly, slowly, they are turning pale. Rubbing the redness out of them.

–*Elizabeth*– she says so quietly. Her voice so small that I almost don't hear it. Then she pulls her hands away and covers her mouth because she doesn't think she should say anything. She is so pretty. the way she's sitting there. Pretty name too. I tell her it's pretty and she looks up at me, looks me in the eyes for the first time.

–*Thanks*– she mumbles and puts her hands back into mine so I can breathe warm air on them again.

I ask her how old she is and she tells me she is 13. I know she's not. I know she's much younger. I know because her hands fit so small in mine. Because her eyes still sparkle like a little kid's. I know she is lying but I don't blame her. I would've lied too. Later, she tells me she's 11. I don't know if that is a lie too. But it doesn't matter. I play along. I tell her I believe.

–*You can stay with me if you want.*– I tell her anything she wants to hear because she's so young. Because her eyes are so scared and I've seen it before and it breaks my heart.

I'm blowing on her hands and she is beginning to shake. She tries to pull her hands away but I hold on. –*Don't, it's okay*– I tell her. She stops trying to get away and I bring her hands to my face. her sleeves slip over her wrists.

The skin is all purple and bruised. it's the light. has to be. I stare longer. turn her hands over and the marks don't go away. Elizabeth looks down. sees what I'm looking at and pulls her hands away. ashamed.

My mouth is open. I want to close it but I can't. I can't because she is not lost. Her parents are not outside looking for her. No one is looking for her. No one that she wants to find her. She's actually one of us. a streetkid.

She's getting up. I frightened her. Her eyes say so. say she hasn't slept for days. all pink around the edges of her blue eyes.

–*Don't go*– I say and she stops. I'm surprised at how much I want this child to stay with me. –*Don't go, it's okay.*–

She sits back down beside me. I hear Lily laugh some-where behind us but it is as if no one else exists. Elizabeth has her hands folded behind her back. I don't want to believe anything bad. that anything bad could happen to this girl. so I ask. –*Did you hurt yourself?*–

Elizabeth shakes her head. moves her hands one on top of the other, then puts them in her pockets and I can see her fingers move like tiny spiders under the fabric.

–*Who hurt you?*– who would? who would do such a terrible thing? the sound of my voice is angry. I can feel the heat in my mouth.

When she answers, I feel things escaping from me. breath. hope. everything that makes me think that maybe the world is a nice place to live. when she says –*sometimes, my dad*– and shrugs her shoulders, it makes me believe that demons are real. and if I ever found them I would kill.

I reach out for her hands again. so that she's not ashamed. so that she knows I will protect her and make it better if she lets me.

–*Do you want to stay with me?*– I ask her.

–*I don't want nothing*– she whispers. She means it to sound brave, but it doesn't. says it with her mouth barely open. Her two front teeth a little bigger than the rest. It makes her look even younger, I guess. Like that song. I can only think of that song. You know, *my two front teeth . . . all I want for Christmas*. But she has hers. –*I don't want nothing*– she says again as she puts her head down. Puts it against my shoulder. Letting herself fall into my arms. Letting herself fall asleep and my heart melts.

I stroke her hair as she sleeps. My fingers sliding through her tangled long hair. It needs to be brushed. needs to be washed. She smells like piss, but I don't mind. I let her sleep. We can take care of all the rest in the morning.

I had a stray once. about a year ago. cute little gray kitten. No one let me keep it. said it would die. that I wouldn't be able to feed it. It was better off on the streets, I guess. Still it followed me for days after I set it free. It broke my heart when I finally ran away and lost it. I cried every night for weeks. I like to think it was taken in. that it had a family that loved it. that it had its own bed and looked out the window every day, looking for me. waiting for me to come back.

Having Elizabeth around is sort of the same thing. No one wants her around at first. But I'm not going to make the same mistake. no way. they can all go to hell. Elizabeth is going to stay everywhere I stay. She is going to go everywhere I go. They'll just have to get used to it and that's that.

Together, me and Elizabeth had to find a new place. Ty didn't say we had to leave, but I didn't want to stay. I didn't want Elizabeth to stay. I don't like looking for new places.

new abandoned buildings where we can move in without anyone noticing. without anyone caring.

You look for the windows. look to see if the windows are boarded up. if the door is boarded up. That's how we find a place. That's how we know it's empty. that it's a squat and we can enter without anyone calling the cops.

We found one. We've been staying there for a week. maybe two. It's a tenement over on Avenue C. It wasn't empty. There were already some kids living there. A different crowd than my old place. Not as many people. a little bit younger. more my age. They don't seem to mind us much. We keep pretty much to ourselves. I don't need them to be my friends. I have other friends.

We still need money, though. Everyone needs money. Even though our rooms are free, we still need money. I'm only 15 so I can't get a job. I have no papers. No parents to sign permission. I can't even ask for work because they might get suspicious. might report me or something.

So we get most of our money the way I always have. We go downtown and hold our hands out. mostly to older men. Wall Street types. They are suckers for young girls who look sad enough. they smile when they give you a few quarters.

Personally, I think they do it out of guilt. Somehow they know somewhere they've done something to make it happen. I think it's funny. I don't blame them for anything. I mean, how could anything they'd ever done be responsible for my stepmom being a heartless bitch? these guys, they just think they're more important than they are. I don't mind. they pay well.

Business definitely gets a boost with Elizabeth around. We tell everyone she's my little sister. that our parents threw us out and we have nowhere to go. They buy it every time. the only problem is if sometimes they fall for it too much and point us out to a cop. then we have to run. being underage and all. It's one thing to have old men living on your streets, I guess. It's another thing if people see little girls living on the street. it's not good for tourism.

We almost always get enough change to buy dinner every night. sometimes breakfast too. But only when I let us spend it all and not put any of it away. I'm saving. saving a little each day. trying to get enough to get out of this town. We are going to move to Hollywood. me and Elizabeth. we are going to become movie stars. at least that's what we say. really, I think we would be happy just being in the woods or something. somewhere else. The city kind of gets to you after a while.

–Isn't that Jef?–

I look down the street. I don't see anyone at first, but sure enough it's him. *–Hey Jef!–* I wave him over. I haven't seen him in a few days. He looks pretty bad. pale, you know? says he's been at a party uptown. ended up sleeping on the street. It was too far to walk all the way back to the Village that late at night. or he was just too lazy. I teased him a little about it. He laughs. says I should stop being such a mom. It is good to see him smile. I miss him now that we don't live in the same place.

–Hey, you girls wanna go have some fun?– Why not? It's Saturday. no suits in town, which means no money to be made. nothing to be gained by standing around.

We meet up with some people in Washington Square. It's a little bit warmer out now that spring is around the corner. You see more people once it gets nice out. People come out of hibernation. Scott is there. Thinner than ever. So thin I can see his skeleton under his shirt. can see each bone in his skull. He isn't with Lily. they're in a fight. They do that every once in a while, but it always works out.

There are a couple of other kids I know there too. Jay. He is my age. He is so funny. He always makes everyone laugh. But he gets kind of shy around me. I think he likes me. I think that's cute.

Marc is there too. He's been around a lot more since that first night. That night I first met Elizabeth. He folded himself into the group just like that. I don't mind him as much. He's harmless. I still don't trust him, though. you can't trust someone with eyes like his. just the way it goes.

I see Eva coming over. She's pretty cool. And gorgeous! All the guys are in love with her. she knows it. She knows how to handle it too. She's moving in on Scott. She always does when he and Lily are split up. She'll never learn, I guess.

I'm in a good mood. Everyone is. even Elizabeth. She's beginning to feel okay around everyone. Some of them were even sort of okay with her around too. The girls mostly. Eva likes her. Likes to tease her like she's our little sister or something. I mean, it still isn't perfect. There's still some tension. I mean, Jef likes her. So does Scott, I guess. But Ty still isn't okay with it. He still thinks she's too young to be on the streets. that she should go home, or to a foster home or something. I don't think it helps that she's still scared of him. that she bites her lip whenever he does try to speak to her. But none of that matters now.

Right now we're happy. The sun is warm, and we are all happy.

Eric knows this rich kid that lives over in the West Village. The kid's parents are out of town. He is letting everyone stay there. like a sleepover or something. We are all going there now to meet him. to meet Eric. Normally I don't like the rich kids that hang out with us. They are always trying to act cool. like our life is so glamorous or something. But when they have sleepovers, I'm like the others. the rich kids are my best friends in the whole wide world then.

The place is real nice. A whole brownstone over on Christopher Street. trees and everything. we can hear the music from a few houses down. We know we're in the right place then.

Jef rings the bell but the door is open. we go in. I don't think they're going to hear it anyway. the doorbell. We see Eric. he is asleep on the couch. napping. Ty is in the kitchen. cooking. it smells nice. like garlic or something. smells like a home, you know. that family smell. just nice is all.

It isn't as crowded as I expected. Other than them and us, there's Billy. the Prince. the boy who lives here. and two other guys I've never seen before in my life. turns out they are Billy's friends. they all go to Dalton. a rich kids' private school uptown. This annoying girl Candy is there too. She's my age and a slut! She is hanging all over Billy. I guess she thinks he'll marry her or something. hoping anyway. I know she's using him. she isn't nice to anyone if she doesn't think there's something in it for her.

It's like everything stops for a second when I walk in. or not everything, just me. I stop. Everything else moves around me as I stare up at the ceiling. The ceiling seems to keep going. Goes all the way up to the sky because of the stained glass skylight at the top of the house that showers light in. And I think this is the most special place I've ever been. I feel like Cinderella or something. Or like I'm playing Cinderella because it can't be anything more than playing. It can never be for real. This castle. It can never be mine for real.

Room after room is filled with fancy furniture. antique glass ornaments that shine like crystals. So delicate I'm afraid to breathe too hard. heavy oak tables that glow like the tables in pledge commercials, or pine sol, or whatever. I can see myself in the tabletop. trapped in the wood. and

37

that's the only way I'll ever be able to live in this house. as a prisoner trapped in the wood. never free to wander around. to have extravagant dinner parties in the grand dining room with friends that are doctors or professors, or other occupations that let you buy these things that are all around me right now.

I grab a seat on the couch before they're all taken. Eva takes the other one. Tosses her head back. Her short hair stays perfectly still. Ladies first.

Eric sits straight up when Elizabeth jumps in his lap. I can't stop laughing. I think he is really in pain but he laughs it off. –*What the fuck's this? It's like a female invasion for christ's sake.*–

I see Ty look out from the kitchen. I think at first he's going to be annoyed. like Elizabeth is proving what a little kid she really is. But Ty just calls in from the kitchen –*Hey what do you know? Eric finally scored.*–

He comes into the living room with a big plate in his hands. Good! I'm starving. but I'm wrong, it wasn't garlic, or onions, or anything at all that I smelled. It isn't anything I can eat. just chemicals. oh well. I'll find something to eat later.

Ty has scored some Special K. a whole bunch. everyone's eyes light up. Not mine, though. I don't want any. it's not like I'm a baby or anything. I'm not an angel. but. I don't know. it's just. well, it's better to stay clean. I don't want to get stuck on the streets my whole life. that's all. I don't mind really that everyone else is high. they'll do their thing. I'll do mine. it's okay.

Ty pushes the powder into little lines. one for everyone. Billy goes first. He paid for it. He's the prince with all the gold. He gets everything first and that is how it goes. I watch the powder disappear like magic. That always makes me laugh. watching things disappear like that I mean. it is so silly to watch.

I look over at Elizabeth. she is watching too. I already passed. said –*no thanks*– and waved my hand. Ty holds the tray in front of her now. –*It's your lucky day little lady. Ladies first. Youngest first. Those are the rules.*– I don't want her to. to take any, I mean. I don't want to treat her like a baby in front of everyone either, but she's looking at me. asking. I shake my head, real quick. my lips curl up kind of like my mother's used to when she was mad at me. I don't say anything but my whole body is telling her –*No.*–

Ty is looking at her. Smiling with his crooked teeth. He is looking at her like it's some kind of test. Like somehow this is going to prove if she's just a little kid or if she belongs with us. Staring. Raising his eyebrows like he's giving a 5-year-old candy or something.

She doesn't take it.

I think she wants to. or she thinks she wants to anyway. I think she just wants Ty to accept her. She still gets really anxious around people. like she's not sure how to act. Taking that junk would only make it worse! I'm worried enough as it is. worried she's going to freak out and want to leave. worried even more that she's going to sniff a line of powder up her nose. but she doesn't. I'm glad. That's the last thing I need. to be nursing her all day. She frowns. turns her nose up. like a little kid that doesn't want to eat something she should. She looks so funny. We all laugh. even Ty. she laughs too because he does. because it seems she's passed his test.

I lean back on the sofa. watching. I feel for Elizabeth's hand. I hold it tight. Everyone has gotten real quiet. slow. their voices are slow. I listen. The sofa is nice. luxurious. I'm tired suddenly. I can't feel my fingers. The music is just right. sounds like the ocean. all around me. I let it in. drifting in and out. tired.

*　　*　　*

I spend most of the day on that couch. sleeping. losing track of time. of people.

I'm not sure when I let go of Elizabeth's hand but I do. when I'm sleeping, I guess. Eva says Elizabeth went into the bedroom to lie down. that was hours ago. I should go check on her. make sure nothing's wrong. Besides, it's getting boring in here. everyone's in their own drugged world anyway. lost to reality. I'm left out of it. Doesn't bother me. them having fun. it doesn't bother me. just boring is all.

I get up. jump up actually. kind of startle everyone. They're all so still, you know. like statues or something. I forget. no sudden movements and that stuff. –*I'm going to find the baby*– I say. I shouldn't have called her that. just trying to sound cool, I suppose. but I shouldn't have. I take it back.

Jay looks at me as I walk by him. Looks at me like only a boy could look at me. with those puppy eyes. He offers to help me. I tell him nevermind. I'm a big girl. I can do it all by myself. teasing him. but it isn't easy. I mean, of course I want him to come. it's cute that he asks. really sweet. But he

41

can't. It is Elizabeth. It's private. I don't know him well enough for that. not yet anyway.

There's so many doors upstairs. I feel dizzy. they all look the same. like each room is an identical toybox filled with wonderfully different things. but I don't want any of them, really. I just want to find Elizabeth.

I think I open every door except the right one. that makes me laugh. I am laughing so hard I don't notice Elizabeth is crying at first. I don't know why, but I was afraid it was something like this. that being at a party would scare her. that it was too much, too soon.

I sit down on the edge of the bed. her head is turned away from me. She looks so funny in that big bed. lost in all that space. a baby bird in a giant nest and all the other birds have flown away. left her there. *–Fend for yourself–* they called as they took off but she can't fly. she still needs to be looked after. to be wrapped up and kept safe and warm and I want to be the one to do it, so I sit on the bed beside her. put my arms on hers and try to absorb some of her tears away.

–Gretchen?– She's the only one that calls me that. probably because she's the only one younger than me. I can

hear the snot in her throat. the tears in her mouth. the sound is like the saddest song I've ever heard. and I want to be able to wave my hand and make it all go away. to give her a new past with happy memories, but I can't. I can't and that makes me helpless. knowing I can't make her feel better but knowing I have to try.

–*What's the matter, squirt? is something wrong?*– I feel so stupid asking. so useless.

–*No. Not really.*– but she starts to really cry then. because everything's wrong. crying because we're kids that have no home. because she's 11 years old and afraid of her shadow, of the moon, of anything that moves. –*I don't like everyone looking at me. I don't want them to look at me, Gretchen, I don't. why do they?*–

I gently let my hand play with her hair. soothing her like a cat. petting her behind her ears. –*they aren't. not really. you just think they are.*–

–*I don't like it here*– she says.

It's getting dark outside. I can see it outside the window. the light's fading in the window. it's almost purple. I point it out to her. –*Isn't it pretty?*–

43

–my mom had curtains like that.–

I look at her. surprised. not sure how to answer her, but she's not paying attention anymore. Her eyes are far away.

–You want to leave?– I ask her. Selfishly, I hope she doesn't. that she will be okay in a minute because I want to stay.

She doesn't say anything. keeps her hands close to her mouth, staring out the window. She's not crying anymore. She's not anything. no expression. like she's hollow inside and I hate it! I want Elizabeth back. happy Elizabeth. I can't stand the silence.

I tug on her braids trying to get her to react. She pushes me away. I tickle her for that. tickle her even though she squirms away. She tries but she can't help it. It's working! me. I am making her feel better because she is laughing. I'm not helpless because she smiles like sunshine. like big clouds and I think maybe I will be able to take care of her after all.

–C'mon– I say. *–Let's go downstairs.–*

But it's too soon. I get carried away in thinking how much a few words and some tickling could accomplish, because she still feels the same inside. She sniffs. *–I don't wanna–* she says. *–I don't like it here.–*

–We don't have to stay.– I'm not going to make her do anything she doesn't want to. I'm not her babysitter. I'm not going to make rules for her.

–Can we just stay up here? you and me?– she is shy about asking. I tell her I would love that and she kind of smiles, but not really. smiles behind her hand which is near her mouth. Hiding her face in the pillow. Hiding her face behind her hair so that only her eyes shine through it.

I have a plan. something we can do. something without everyone else so she will relax. so she will have a good time. I ask her if she wants to take a shower. They have a fancy rich person's bathroom with hot water and soap and clean towels. I tell her I'll brush her hair. She brightens up. a warm bath! it's irresistible. Beats cold-water showers we take in the vacant lot. that's for sure. *–C'mon!–* Elizabeth finally gets up off the bed, which still looks way, way too big for her to be in.

I call down the stairs that we're taking a shower. *–No boys allowed on the next floor!–* Jef runs halfway up the stairs. I hold my hand out. tell him to stop in the name of

the law. the law's the law. He turns back. only slightly disappointed.

Elizabeth's already in the bathroom when I get in there.
The steam is escaping into the hallway. The water pour-
ing into the drain and I can hear it pitter-patter against the
tiles. I can hear her too. She's singing. at the top of her lungs.
screaming it but all silly. –La, La, Le-La-La-La!– I open the
door and her voice is so loud I almost have to cover my ears.

And I'm laughing. I laugh so hard because I can hardly
see her. The steam is so thick. like a cloud or fog or something. But I can see her. see her streak by. totally naked.
see her only for a second because she's running around
through the steam singing at the top of her lungs. Then
she's gone. There's so much room. The bathroom is HUGE!
twice the size of a normal room in a normal person's house.

She runs up to me. Her little hands are all wet. pressing
on my shirt and now my shirt is all wet. She's laughing too.
laughing with her tongue sliding along the bottom of her
two front teeth.

–*STOP!*– I yell, but it's not convincing because I'm laughing. She's trying to pull my pants off and I'm trying to push her away but she's all slippery. So I tickle her instead and she bends her side away from me. Bends her hips away from my fingers. Finally letting go and running again into the clouds that hang on the tile.

I hear the shower door slide open and closed. Hear her singing in the shower and her feet splashing around. I feel like a princess in a story. standing in this bathroom with its ivory sink and silk curtains. I feel like a princess as I get undressed. as my dirty clothes fall against the gleaming floor.

I follow the sound of her voice through the fog. follow it until I find the sliding door and it slides easily. It's strange, but it doesn't feel weird at all. I mean, it doesn't feel weird at all to be climbing in there where Elizabeth has her eyes closed. the water running over her eyes. over her parted lips. I watch her for a second before I say anything. watch the water fall over her skin. watch her skin where it shows how much younger than me she is. how vulnerable she is and I promise silently to myself to always protect her.

She pretends to not be paying attention. to be rinsing her hair, so I don't expect it when her hands suddenly move from her head. move so fast like a rabbit and splash me and I jump because no matter how much steam there is, the water is still startling the first time it touches me. –*ha, ha!*– she says and I make a face and then we both laugh. laugh as the dirt rinses away from us and travels far away down the drain.

When we're drying off, I see her looking around. Her eyes clean and wide. looking at the fancy soap that is shaped like a unicorn. at the picture made of seashells that hangs over the toilet.

–*It's really nice*– I say.

–*What is?*–

–*This room! It's beautiful.*–

Elizabeth turns her nose up and squints. –*Sort of*– she says with her mouth open. –*It's a little dumb, though.*–

–*What? It's amazing.*– and I'm carrying on like this place is the best place either of us has ever seen. –*how can you say that?*–

Elizabeth shakes her head. –*I dunno. Just reminds me of my house is all.*– and she lets the towel cover her face, dry-

48

ing her forehead and I feel so small. so stupid. but she never likes to talk about that. No one likes to talk about where they came from. I still feel bad. I want to say I'm sorry. But that would only make it worse, so I let it go.

Looking through Billy's mom's closet, I've never seen so many clothes. Glittery dresses and floor length gowns. Furs. Elegant vests and scarves made of silk. Labels with French, fancy sounding names I can't pronounce. From one end to the other, it's like the racks at a department store. Shoes in every color. High heels. Low heels. No heels. Some with straps, some with buckles. I try on like fifteen million things. hope Billy doesn't mind. I guess I don't really care even if he does. I'm having fun. After all, it is a party isn't it?

I'm set on a small black dress. it looks good on me. so good I don't mind seeing myself in the mirror. I can't take my eyes off myself. I look really good. Elizabeth agrees with me. says I look important or something.

That's what I could be. if this was all mine. the clothes. the house. the money. I could be someone important.

Someone who people look at and don't think is worthless. I could hide in these clothes. hide the fact that I'm just another runaway. just another stupid white-trash girl who isn't going to go very far. But forget all that. Not tonight. Tonight is for fun. If I can't hide in these clothes forever, at least I can hide for tonight.

–*What are you going to wear?*– I ask Elizabeth. She looks around, then she points to my t-shirt. the one with the daisy on it. my happy shirt. –*Sure, why not?*– and she jumps up. she's so happy I think she might explode. truth is, she looks really cute in it. I put a pink silk scarf around her head and tie it under her chin. Perfect. I go into the closet one more time. come out wearing a waist length fur coat. now we're ready.

I grab Elizabeth by the hand. –*Let's go downstairs.*– and she follows along. Everyone is staring at us. We look great! We know it. What did they think? Did they think the dirt was natural?

Eva runs over to us. her short hair pushed behind her ear, which makes her look like a boy. She's all excited. I feel like a thousand dollars. She's gushing about how wonderful we look. –*My god!*– she says like she sometimes does. She wants her turn next. She wants to transform herself into something else like we have. She's already up the stairs. Scott's following her. I guess him and Lily must really be over. or they will be now. if she ever finds out, I mean.

Billy doesn't seem to mind that I took the clothes from his mom's closet. never says so anyway. he's too fucked up to care. most of them are. I don't mind. I move like a princess among them. like in a dream. them all in slow-motion. I glide through them. shining. like I'm in color and they're all in black & white.

A whole new group of people has shown up. I don't know most of them. recognize their faces, though. from the neighborhood. I've seen them. It doesn't matter. Everyone is happy. Everyone is friends for tonight at least. Tomorrow may be different. But for now, now we're all just having a good time on someone else's money.

It's a little more lively now that Jay has found the liquor cabinet. seems to mix well with the other drugs they're doing. gives them energy anyway. It is also making them pass out. There are kids falling down everywhere. The music is so loud I can hardly hear anything. Billy has a set of turntables set up. All the guys want to show off. Typical.

It's great, though. like a real party at a club or something. In a little while there are so many people, they might as well charge people to get in.

I'm in the kitchen. I must be a little drunk because I'm hanging out with Candy. Candy, who I don't even really like. I don't drink much. hardly ever. actually this is only like the third time in my life. Candy seems okay when I'm like this. like she's my best friend. She is making fun of Billy's rich kid friends. They don't know what to say to her. She can care less. Besides, she is with Billy. She's untouchable. He is too wrecked to notice she's pissing off all his friends. She loves every minute of it.

I see Jef making out with some girl I've never seen before. He looks pretty bad. can't keep his eyes open. his skin looks all pale and everything. She looks worse. bone thin. her hair is thin and falling out. She's all holding on to him. if she were to let go, I think she'd fall away and disappear like a ghost. She's so pathetic. ugly too. He'll never learn, I guess. Always the same thing with him. If I remember, I'll have to tease him about it in the morning.

Everyone is kind of out of control. kind of fucked up. having fun. too much maybe. being annoying. I want to get out for a little bit. get away. just for a little bit.

Somehow, I end up with Jay. I love how shy he is when I come up to him. I want to go for a walk. I want him to take me. It's pretty easy to convince him. it's never really that hard. a smile. a blink of the eyes. that's about all. especially if you're wearing a short dress that costs more money than either of us has ever seen our whole entire lives.

–Take me for a walk? Please.–

We are out the front door before he can even say yes or no.

–What are we doing out here anyway? Where're we going?–

I know better than to give him an answer. secrets are a girl's best friend. secrets are how you get boys to do what you want them to. *–Shut up and put your arm around me. Don't you trust me?–* It's kind of sweet how clumsy he is. I bet he's never even kissed a girl the way he acts. that's sweet, though. I'd hate him if he was all tough and all. all showing off or whatever.

We get pretty strange looks. I mean, here I am dressed up all high class. clean. elegant. like I just stepped out of a

Lexus or something. Jay looks like shit. His eyes are so bloodshot they'd probably put him in the hospital if they thought about it for a second. His clothes are dirty too. he is dirty. smells a little too. but that's who he is. that's who I am. he's perfect. At least tonight he seems that way.

We stumble along each block. nearly falling down every step we take. I can't stop laughing. The cars are going by so fast it makes me dizzy. so many people. It's hard to see straight. I've never felt so good in my life. so totally free from everything. I think that must be what Ty meant when he told me he wanted to be on the streets. That this feeling is the most wonderful thing about belonging to the street. nights like this. nights when nothing matters, when anything can happen.

After a while, I figure we've been sitting here for hours. probably not, though. in this little playground in Soho. sitting on a wooden jungle gym painted yellow. No one else is here. It's nice. I made Jay chase me here for about four blocks. he didn't catch me until we got here. making as much noise as we wanted.

–*You ever wonder where you'll end up?*–

–*No.*–

–Liar!–

–Okay. yeah. But . . . I mean. Well, I don't want to talk about that now. You know?– That's okay with me. I don't either, I just wanted to ask.

–Yeah, maybe. But you know what I do wonder?–

–No. what?–

–I wonder when you're going to kiss me.–

He climbs up to where I am. pretty fast. fast as he can. He sure loses his shyness pretty quick. I think we're going to fall for sure. but I hold on. hold on to him and he holds on to me. and just before I close my eyes, I see three lights spark to life in the Empire State Building, like stars just for me. my mind is made up. there really is no choice after that. I've settled on which building is my favorite, once and for all.

Someone is screaming. She is crying. or has been. her face is wet. I have no idea what is happening. where I am. the place is a mess. it is Billy's of course. it takes me a moment is all. There is a lot of screaming and yelling. My head is pounding. Jay is still asleep next to me on the couch.

It's Elizabeth who's crying. her head buried in my side. she won't talk. won't tell what's going on. Eva is running down the stairs, into the room. She is screaming too. yelling at me to get up. that I should, that I need to go upstairs. to hurry. She is talking so fast I can only make out every other word.

–*What the FUCK is going on!*– I yell. Everyone is freaking out. –*What happened? Did someone die? Fucking tell me what's going on! Please.*–

–*You better get upstairs*– Eva says. slower this time. –*I think they're going to kill him.*– She gathers Elizabeth in her arms. I look down at her. I see her face for the first time. see the bruise around her eye. I scream.

Tripping up the stairs, a thousand and one things race through my mind. I'm panicking. I still don't know for sure what happened, but I have a pretty good idea, though, and that is worse than knowing.

It's one of Billy's private school friends. He tried to do something with her. he tried real hard. Jef and Eric are holding him down while Ty beats the shit out of him.

I can't feel my hands. His mouth is bleeding really bad. His eyes are half closed already. I'm not sure what Eva thought I was going to do. Maybe she just wants to make sure I see the bastard get what he deserves. But I'm so mad I can't see. seeing red. that's what they call it. that's what I am. Seeing red.

Billy is trying to stop them. yelling and everything. seems like there is noise coming from everywhere. The guy keeps trying to break free but Scott has him pretty good. Jay comes running into the room then too. He goes after the kid who did it. All of them start beating on him at once. kicking him when he's on the floor. I see his teeth fall out. I see him spit up blood each time they kick him in the stomach.

Billy finally breaks free and runs into the next room. Scott chases him, but Billy locks the door behind him. We know he's calling the police. that he's terrified.

I jump on top of the kid on the floor. start hitting him over and over. I'm saying things without even knowing what I'm saying.

They are just like everyone else. want us around for their amusement is all. like we're fucking circus freaks or something. just lowlifes. we mean nothing to them. there for them to use, that's what they think.

Jef is pulling me off. *–Come on, Chan, we gotta get out of here now. Come on!–* have to run out of there before the police come. the ambulance. I can already hear the sirens racing through the city. the sound of police engines and cop voices. I hate them all so much! hate them with every breath.

I hate myself for thinking they really wanted us there. that they were our friends. that none of it had a price. the house, the free stuff. I hate the stupid black dress that I am wearing. I hate the trees in front of Billy's beautiful front window. hate everything right then. that's why I do it. why I pick up the rock and throw it through the glass. watching it shatter all over the carpet, the sofa, the coffee table, and everything else.

Elizabeth is still crying. Ty is carrying her in his arms and she looks weaker than anything. He has to carry her. She isn't that big and we have to get out of there fast.

We're huddled together on the floor of some place that seems familiar but that could be because these squats are all the same. bombed out. smelling of sewers and trash. no lights to see anything either.

Ty says we got to stay here a while. *–The police will look for us. we're important now.–* It makes me so mad. beat up a rich kid and suddenly you're alive to them. searching for us like criminals. WANTED. all of us. even Elizabeth who I have to take to the bathroom because she doesn't want to be left alone.

–He told me nobody'd believe me– she says to me. *–I told him I didn't want to do nothing and he said if I didn't he would tell the cops I tried to steal stuff.–*

I'm so mad I don't say anything. terrified to hear Elizabeth go on because I don't yet know how bad it's going to be.

–I didn't want him to call the cops! I didn't!– she's crying.

–Did he touch you?–

She shakes her head. *–I didn't let him. So he punched me.–*

Right then, I hope he's dead. in a hospital room with doctors not trying to save him until he's completely dead.

–It's my fault– she says under her swollen lip. *–my dad always said it was my fault. that's why it happened to me.–*

We are both crying now.

–Don't say that. Don't ever say that again!– I brush the hair away from her face. make her look me in the eyes and say it. actually say it. *–It's not your fault.–*

We are completely alone. alone in a small room in a strange building and we are both filled with each other's secrets.

–Gretchen?– she looks up at me. Her hair is matted to her forehead again. black hair stuck in her wet eyelashes. we are lying down on the old couch. using it as a bed. Early evening light through the window. dim. soft. Her hair is

soft. I run my hand through it. Her hair is black like mid-night against my fingers.

–Gretchen? Will you promise not to leave me?– She blinks when she asks. turns away because she is shy about asking.

–I promise– and I wipe the corner of my eye because I don't want her to see me crying. Because she has been so brave and I must be brave too. I promise her that I will never let her out of my sight again. I will kill myself if anything ever happens to her again.

–Gretchen?– she whispers when I'm done talking and I make a noise so she knows I'm listening. She doesn't look at me when she says it. She doesn't even really say it all the way but I hear it anyway. *–I love you–* she says before she turns over and closes her eyes.

That night she tells me about her dad. when we are alone. tells me everything. how he used to burn her with cigarettes and beat her. I mean it when I say I'll kill him if I ever find out where he is. I will.

I let her fall asleep in my arms and I wonder how we ever ended up here. why things always have to happen. things that are bad. why they always happen to people who don't deserve them. I never asked for this life. Elizabeth didn't either. I wonder if that even matters for anything at all.

In my dream I'm an angel. with pretty wings. pretty white dress. I'm pretty too. prettier than I could ever be. No one can see me. jumping from the top of buildings. I fall. so close to the cars below that I can reach out and touch them if I want. I don't. I don't want to wake up. I fly back up instead. I fly so high I'm scared. it's so easy. I could just keep going. higher and higher. never come back.

I'm crying. It's so beautiful. The stars are so bright, I can't see. It's so quiet. so cold. I'm smiling. The city's getting smaller. far below me. so far. I'm floating. I can't feel my body. I laugh, but I can't hear my voice. I'm happy. swimming with the stars. I'm the luckiest person alive.

I wish the feeling would never go away. that it would stay even when I wake up. It never does. That's okay. It wouldn't be fair. It wouldn't be a dream then. I hold on as long as I can, though. It's selfish maybe. I know Elizabeth is waiting for me to get up. she always does. Just a few more minutes, okay? I'll be there soon. Just a minute longer. One last leap. one last fall. let me go. just once more please?

But it's our stop. Elizabeth shakes me. she doesn't want to miss it. I have to get up. The doors are going to close. –*Okay, I'm coming!*– I just want her to stop pulling at me. I push her away. the doors close behind us. the train pulls away.

She's mad at me. I can tell. I don't care. I'm not exactly in the best mood either. This day was ruined as soon as it started. It was supposed to be so perfect.

We've been planning this for weeks. have saved up for it. I'm taking Elizabeth shopping. I'm sick of seeing her in the same old thing. that boring *New York Dolls* t-shirt that Lily gave her. I'm sick of her acting like it's the coolest thing she ever saw. It's just a stupid t-shirt. I don't even know who they are. no way she does. It doesn't fit her anyway. It's way too big.

Ever since we started hanging out with Lily all the time, that's all Elizabeth ever talks about. Lily this. Lily that. –*isn't Lily so cool?*– and it's always a different story. –*hey, guess what Lily did? She told off this woman in the store and then know what? We got everything for free!*– yeah, cool! She's a criminal. I mean, I pretend to be happy when Elizabeth tells me these things. Pretend to be happy. I am happy, you know, happy Elizabeth is making friends. But I'm sick of it. If Lily's so great, go wake her up every day! See how cool she is then! I don't know. It's not that I don't like Lily. I like her a lot. It's just, I don't know. I don't know, it's nothing. I'm overreacting, I guess.

But Elizabeth is getting *too* close to Lily. I mean, starting to act like her. to do things that Lily would do, but that I never thought Elizabeth could. Sure, Lily stealing from some jerk on the street, that's not hard to imagine. it's not even imagining. more like it happens all the time. It's fine with me. Fine for her, I mean. but it's not my thing. and it's NOT Elizabeth's either. It can't be. Not if she's gonna be with me.

That's why I'm so pissed. because she did it. The man was just trying to be nice. more than I can say for most of the other assholes. He actually cared. And she stole from him! took his wallet right there in front of me. I saw her do it.

It happened just a little while ago. in the park. We were just minding our own business. watching the sun come up. We were all excited about today, you know. new clothes, shopping and all that. This man came up to us. kind of ugly. more old, really. he was nice and everything. he wasn't a creep. He was asking us if everything was alright. I guess we looked pretty bad. dirty, I mean. We let him sit down for a minute. no harm in that. Until he got real nosy.

I did my best to convince him we were fine. *–just waiting for our parents–* just in case he got too concerned and squealed on us or something. You have to be careful. Didn't matter though. he wasn't buying it. but he wasn't looking to rat us out either. gave me a couple of dollars even.

It was sticking out of his pocket. his wallet. after he put it away. I saw it. I saw Elizabeth's eyes light up. the thief! Lily's little thief. I saw her little hands reach for it. they looked so small. so greedy. I gave her such a mean look. It didn't stop her. He left not long after that.

I didn't speak to her. Sure, I ran away with her. I was mad but I wasn't going to let her get caught. I'm not evil. She said she was sorry. She just wanted us to have enough money so we could get something nice. *–We already had enough!–* We're not criminals. Nothing we could get would ever make me feel good about it.

–Okay, but now we have more. Right?–

–Don't you get it? That's why people look at us like that. Like we're nothing. I hate when they look at us like that. I hate when they look at you like that! You're better than that. Don't give them a fucking reason. Don't make them right. They can never be right. You understand?–

–*But Lily does it*– Elizabeth says just like a brat. Half smiling like it makes it okay because someone else does it too.

–*Lily!*– I scream. I'd had it. –*Fuck Lily! Lily also has a rich daddy who would come get her out of trouble whenever she called. Lily's not on the streets because she needs to be. You get that? You want the police to call your daddy? Have him come and take you home?*– and I bit my lip because I shouldn't have said that. But she needs to understand the difference.

She cried. for a while. a long while. I was pretty mean, I guess. I felt bad. not too bad, though. I'm still really mad at her. Not that I don't know why she did it. I do. but that doesn't make it okay. I mean I don't want to be her mom or anything. but there are rules. Some things you just can't do. no matter how much you want to. no matter how easy it is. You just can't.

It's so frustrating. she's walking so slow now. she's doing it on purpose just to make me mad. We came all the way out here for this? I'm not going to spend the entire day doing this. back and forth. not talking.

I'm going to kill her if she stops one more time! She keeps stopping. then I have to stop and she walks past me.

–*Stop!*– I'm not playing games. I'm so sick of this. She reaches into her jeans. takes out all those small bills. tens. fives. singles. all crumpled into a ball.

–*Here! I don't want it.*–

That much money looks silly in her hands. they're so small. must be $200 easy. It's hard to stay mad at her for so long. really hard. because when she frowns I just want to laugh. but I can't. I have to stay mad.

–*Yeah, well, I don't want it. So there!*–

–*I don't want it either. not if you're going to be so grumpy all day. I said I'm sorry. So here. Take it.*–

–*No.*– I'm going to let her spend it. and I'm going to make sure she feels pretty guilty about doing it.

–*HERE!*–

–*NO! Forget it. I'm not taking it.*–

She tries to put it in my pocket. I block her, though. –*Too slow*– I say. now I'm just teasing her. She's getting pretty angry. she can't get the money in my pocket. I'm smiling. She tries to put the money down my shirt. I'm laughing. she's laughing. She sticks the money down my pants. I scream. we're both laughing pretty good after that.

But I have to stay angry. I take it out. I put it down her shirt. –*I mean it!*– I say. –*I DON'T want it.*–

She looks the other way. opens her hands like a butterfly. the money drops to the ground. I stare at it. She doesn't even look at it again. just keeps walking. It's a lot of money. a lot. maybe I. NO. I can't.

I have to run a few steps. just a few. to catch up. I almost say something. but I don't. I don't know what to say. so I keep walking.

It's driving me crazy! She won't even look at me. This was supposed to be fun. So far, today has been just one big downer. I hate this. maybe I should just go home. I mean, I have other things I could be doing. I don't need this. the silent treatment from a little brat. Okay. So that's not fair. She didn't deserve that. but it is all her fault.

It feels so natural when Elizabeth grabs my hand. I don't even notice it at first. It fits nice there. funny. her hands seemed so small when she held all that money but they're pretty much the same size as mine. She says she's sorry again. means it this time.

–Hey. Don't worry about it, okay?–

Her eyes are red. puffy. she has pretty eyes. I wish I had eyes like hers. so big. so clean and blue. –C'mon. let's get you clothes. pretty clothes.– It was going to be fun. had to be. I mean, what good are we if we can't even have some fun spending money, right? It's a poor girl's dream after all, right?

–Besides– I say –you look like a boy in that shirt. It's such a mean look. You're too cute for it.–

She smiles. It's pretty to see. like the sunshine.

She's looking down at herself. the end of her t-shirt reaches to her knees. she has no chest for it. the collar is way too low. She knows it. It looks horrible on her. At the top of her lungs, she yells –Fuck the New York Dolls!– it sounds so funny coming from her. she has such a little voice. she's so proud of herself. I'm proud of her too. or happy at least. glad she's taking my side again. besides, first store's right around the corner and we got fifty bucks between us.

70

*   *   *

Jay's late as usual. he's always late. every time. every time we've met since he kissed me in the playground as I saw the lights flash on in the Empire State Building. no big deal. I don't mind really. because I think of him kissing me, and I can wait. Besides it's not like he owns a watch or anything. I just wish he was here that's all. These stupid guys wouldn't be talking to us then. They'd leave.

It's on account of our new clothes. clean, new clothes. Now we look like all the other girls here in the park. not dirty clothes to set us apart. to boys we're now approachable. now real people. Great! Hey, gain something lose something. give and take and all that. I *never* should've bought a tank top! creep magnet if ever there was one, that's for sure.

These guys just can't take a hint. They're older. sixteen or so. Dorks. desperate, obviously. I'm even acting like a royal bitch to them but they don't get it. We're not even listening. I don't even think Elizabeth knows what they're talking about. what they're getting at I mean. Because they're not even talking about anything. just stupid stuff.

I wish Jay would show up. These guys aren't going to leave until he shows. I'm not leaving. I mean, this is where we're meeting him. I can't. –*That looks nice.*– I've decided to completely ignore them and just talk to Elizabeth. She does look nice. We bought her a summer dress. It's getting way too hot out for jeans. especially when you don't have any air-conditioning. when you got no air-conditioned place to go either. like a job, or a restaurant.

–*Thanks. It's my favorite.*– We bought two outfits each. that should last us until winter. then we can always wear what we wore last winter. Or buy something new if we decide to spend some of our money. But I am trying to save it. all of it. I want to get out of this city someday. sooner rather than later. I want to get out of this city before winter. If we can anyway.

–*Chan, do you think I should cut my hair?*– twirling the ends into her mouth. She's finally catching on. If we keep talking about girl stuff, these losers'll get the idea. get lost.

–*Sure! I think you should cut it real, real short at the top and keep it real, real long in the back.*– She takes the piece out of her mouth. looks at it. She looks like she's really thinking about it. shrugs her shoulders and everything. I can't help it. I can't hold it in any longer and we both start giggling.

72

Dork Number One and Dork Number Two are dumber than I thought. They're whispering to each other. I thought they were asking each other if they should leave. I would've been if I was them. But I guess I was giving them a bit too much credit.

–*Hey Chan?*– the taller, uglier one says to me. I mean, it's hard not to laugh and all. –*you wanna go back to your place or something?*– My eyes go so wide they'd probably fly out of my face if that were possible. Where did these guys come from? And how do they always find *me,* that's what I'd like to know.

–*Give us a break!*–

I turn back to Elizabeth. making such a funny face at her that she starts laughing. The other guy, the younger, cuter guy, comes closer so he can sit next to her. I guess he thought this was first grade. you know, like if a girl laughs at you that's because she likes you?

–*What?*– he asks. –*Do you live far away or something?*–

Elizabeth makes a face. all snotty and stuff. rolling her eyes, shaking her head and everything. –*We don't even have a home!*– she says.

–Really? That's so cool.–

–FUCK off, will you?– Jesus! Yeah. We're sooooo glamorous, why don't you just take a picture and show all your friends. Tell all your dork friends how cool the squatter chicks are. I push his skinny arm off her. push him away. *–FUCK off, loser.–*

–Careful, I think she's mad– the other starts in again with that ugly laugh. What? now he thinks he's cool again? Where does he get off?

–Jay!– Elizabeth jumps up and runs over to him. gives him a great big hug. like a little kid. She's really happy to see him. I get up slowly. I see the two guys talking. walking away. FINALLY.

–What's going on, squirt?– Jay's so relaxed. so easygoing. so late. It's just like him. *–Hey, Chan. Who were they? Anyone I know?–*

–Hope not. Just some losers.–

–Who? Those guys?– he ruffles Elizabeth's hair. He's looking kind of dirty. cute, though. *–They bothering you, squirt? Want me to kick their ass?–*

–*No, they're harmless*– I say. He was just joking anyway. couldn't hurt them if he tried. He's only my size after all. I don't think he would have even if he could. He'd rather make jokes about it. you know, end the situation that way? whatever. doesn't matter to me. I'm glad he's here, though. glad to see him.

–*So. What do you girls want to do?*– I have no idea. don't even care. He takes my hand. We'll find something to do. always do. If not, we'll do nothing at all. That would be fine with me too. It's such a nice night out. the sky painted purple. perfect breeze. let's walk for hours. for days. just keep going. just as long as we all stay together. that would be nice. like a dream. my dream. all for me.

He passes. quick. It's just out of the corner of my eye that I see him. only for a second. but I've been seeing him more and more. Strangers. not the same one. Like this time, he's a different one than I saw yesterday, or the day before. different from the one I saw two days before that even. But they all look the same. they all look like my father. Some are a little older. a little fatter. But at a glance, I really think it's him. It never is.

Sometimes I think I mistake people for him because maybe I don't remember what he looks like. maybe these guys look nothing like him and I wouldn't even know. It's been a few years after all. he could be a hundred pounds heavier. or bald. or I don't know. He could live in China or something. I would have no idea.

That bothers me sometimes. I mean, he's not a bad guy. I love him. I do. really. But I hate him for not choosing me. He picked her. He loved her more than me. or he wouldn't have picked her. he would've picked me. I'd be home right now, watching tv, lying on the couch smiling at the Bless this Mess sign over the mantel. That wouldn't be so bad. It'd be kind of nice, actually. as long as she wasn't there.

I think about calling him sometimes. I guess he'd like to hear from me. hear I'm okay. It's nice to think he would anyway.

I could pick up the phone right now and like magic, BOOM, there he'd be on the other end. I have the number memorized. I mean, I haven't dialed it in years but there it is. automatic. right there in my head. you dial the first number and the rest just come.

I can't bring myself to do it. I panic every time I pick up the phone. Anyway, he probably has a new number by now. but that's just me talking myself out of it. giving up. I mean, what if he's been too scared to change it? too scared I'd call one day and not be able to reach him? Thinking like that makes me sad. I don't like to be sad. I'd rather be happy.

Whatever, it's not like he ever came looking for me. I never saw *my* face on any milk carton. If he did, he didn't look hard enough. not when I was freezing my ass off. lonely. scared out of my mind. He didn't look hard enough then. when I was 13, scared of my own shadow. He didn't look hard enough when I was in his own fucking house. I guess I never really expected him to look. I just would have hoped he would've.

So I decided to not look for him anymore. not in the faces of strangers. not through the phone lines. through the operators. not even in my dreams.

The next person I see and I think it might be my dad, I'm going to look the other way. I'm not going to turn around. to get a better look. I don't want him to break my heart anymore.

We took up with Lily about two weeks ago. Where we had been staying was getting crowded. it always gets crowded in summer. More kids run away in the summer. new kids. new faces you've never seen before. faces you won't see for long. not long enough to get to know them anyhow. you know, they're just weekend kids. the ones that always go home when they run out of money. or get bored. I didn't want to be around them. Lily's place was much better. pretty empty. We moved right in.

Eric's living there now too. He looks so different from the first time I met him. That California tan, that California accent. both gone. He and Lily got together once Scott and her were completely over. The change has been good for Elizabeth. she seems much happier. not as shy. Eric's been good for her too. she likes having a guy around. makes her feel safe, I guess.

This new place is not in a great neighborhood. it's way out on Avenue D. nobody comes out this far. it's scarier than the rest of the avenues, because the streets are empty.

79

You only see shadows in doorways or windows. Sometimes you see a flash of light and some smoke, and then the smell of drugs because the junkies live out here where no one will bother them.

I get used to it, though. Streetkids can get used to anything, I guess. Besides, it's quiet. I like that about this neighborhood.

I've got a lot of money saved now. Almost $700. that's enough for a lot of things. enough to get us out of here by bus. plane even. enough to get us far away and never come back. but it's not enough of enough. not yet.

Lily and Eric don't know we have any money saved. I made Elizabeth promise not to tell. I mean, Lily's been great to us. Eric too. I feel terrible about lying to them. Well, I'm not really lying. just not telling them everything. It's not that I don't trust them in particular. I guess I just don't trust anyone.

Lily picked some flowers the other day. put them in the window. they look pretty there. I like them. makes me feel like it's a home. She picked them in front of an office building downtown. they're dying now. but still they're pretty. When she brought them home, she was smiling. She didn't look like herself. more like a girl in the movies that just met her first love and is all gushing over him to her friend or sister or somebody. but it had nothing to do with that. it was only the flowers. I asked why they made her so happy. *–I don't know–* she said. *–they make me feel like a normal person.–*

Eric says the police have been shutting down other squats. going in and kicking everyone out. always at night. it must be pretty scary. He says they won't bother over here. That's why he and Lily picked this place out. I wonder how long it will take, though. how long before our home is cleaned out so it can be someone else's.

It's not like it's much of a place. The walls are torn open like ripped sheets. When you walk too fast or when you jump up and down, the whole building seems to shake. I don't know why they'd bother. The cops, I mean. I don't know why they would bother with this place. Still, though, I try not to get too attached. I try not to think of it as a home. But somehow, it's like that. The way we use the holes in the wall to talk to each other through the rooms. The way the stairs are falling down and we sometimes have to jump because the last two stairs can't really support a person.

–Chan, we were thinking about going out, you guys wanna come?–

Lily looks so nice. her hair like that. clipped behind her ears. I look away from the window. the flowers. I look away to look at her. I don't say anything. I'm waiting for her to say where they're going. She was just waiting for my attention. then she'll tell me. I know she will.

–Eric's friend is working at The Continental tonight. Says he can get us in. You guys should come with us. it'll be fun. I promise.–

Why not? I don't say anything, but I nod. getting up. I'm just going through the motions. getting changed and everything. My mind's just not into it. I'm thinking about other things right now. about leaving the city. not coming back. about an open sky that starts at one end and ends at the other. all the stars are there. shining. and trees too. lots of them. me and Elizabeth lying on a blanket somewhere and staring up at them so hard that our eyes are going to burst.

Elizabeth's sleeping on the bed in our room when I go in. it's not really a bed, I guess. not according to the dictionary anyway. just a bunch of old cushions thrown together in the corner. They don't smell or anything. they smell like her. like powder.

I don't really want to wake her up but I'm not going to leave her here alone. I don't want to go but I already said yes. everything looks so nice, so calm. I just want to climb in there next to her. the way the sun is coming in the window before going away.

I put my hand on her hair. she doesn't even flinch. doesn't move a muscle. dreaming of something beautiful, I bet.

–Elizabeth? C'mon, we gotta get ready. You wanna go out?–

The way she moves is so small. so tired and new. She's blinking her eyes. she has such pretty eyes when she's yawning. stretching. I get up to give her room to wake up.

We decide to match tonight. It will be fun. like twins almost. or sisters at the least. Each of us has a skirt on. red. with lots of ruffles. they're costume clothes really. we don't mind. that's what going out's all about. Identical white shirts. sleeveless. We got them when we went shopping last time. we're giggling. looking at ourselves next to each other in the mirror. we look like fairy-tale characters. I want to climb through the mirror and live that life. The one where there's a wolf chasing us but other than that we can be totally happy.

–Oh my god, you two look great! That's fabulous!–

Lily rushes in, putting her hands around our waists and spinning us around. She's really excited. that helps me get excited. I blow myself a kiss in the mirror like a movie star or something. holding my hair up. just like that. like old photographs.

I keep seeing Elizabeth's face peeking into the mirror. dancing around me. I keep switching poses. she's jumping around. Lily is pretending to be an agent or something. *–That's it. Keep it there. That's it. Hold it.–* It's fantastic. them jumping around me. I feel like a star. I'm not even noticing them after a while. I'm looking at myself. my own face. I look beautiful. I've never seen myself like this. must be the way the sun is setting. the way the light is fading in the other room. I think I could watch myself like this until the sun completely goes away and then it's dark. then I'll go back to just being me.

It's so crowded out. The streets are filled with people. that's New York, I guess. people from here and there. from all over the place. I can blend in. move between them and it's like I disappear. the lights from the cars. everyone rushing by. the warm breeze in my hair. smells like the seashore.

I'm going to meet them later. Lily and Eric. Elizabeth. she's going to go with them. I'm going to pick up Jay. Eric said he ran into him today. that he was over on Astor Place. I'll take a chance. nothing to lose really. it's not that far out of the way. right around the corner to be honest. probably doesn't even make sense for them not to come with me. they would've. they asked. but I wanted to go alone. I want to see him smile and know he's smiling just because of me.

There are a lot of people there but I don't see him for sure. Maybe he's there. Stupid traffic light. I have to wait for it to change. tapping my side. my heart's going to jump out of my body. I'm so impatient. so nervous and I have no idea why. I guess I just want Jay to see me looking so good. feeling so good about myself. I'm crossing the street now. The light's changed. I don't see him yet. I can't believe I'm so nervous. falling to pieces. I'm going to crack up laughing as soon as I see him if I don't pull myself together. I have to. That's not what I want him to see. not right now. he's already seen that side of me. I want him to see this side. the strong, beautiful side. I want him to see it before it goes away.

There's no one I know standing in the middle of the square. The square median sits in the middle of the intersections so pedestrians can cross easily. Two avenues going north on each side. two streets going east on the other two sides. cars driving on all sides of me while the people pass. He's not here. I look both ways. I look up. I feel so small. the way the buildings reach up to the sky. they make me feel so little. little shirt and little skirt. I feel so dumb. standing here all alone with everything going by. But I don't leave. don't want to move.

I can't believe how fast things change inside of me. it's so confusing. I wouldn't want Jay to see me right now for a million dollars. part of me wants to run. to run so fast the sidewalk bursts into flames. part of me's afraid I'll miss him. that he's here and I just don't see him. that I'll feel even stupider if I leave and he sees me walking away.

It's like the dream I had the other night. there were these giant scorpions. as big as my hands. They were all swimming around in the toilet. I was afraid they came out of me. I was terrified. Shaking. I wanted to get out of that bathroom faster than anything. But when I did, nothing was better. There were people everywhere. It was a restaurant. It was full. All the people I've ever known were there. talking to each other. No one noticed me. No one said a single word to me. I almost wanted to go back into the bathroom. I couldn't understand what they were all doing there. why they wanted to ignore me. I felt so stupid. I wanted to run. but that wouldn't have made a difference. they were there. they were staying. it was a funeral party for me. the scorpions were trying to tell me that much. I wouldn't listen. I never do. not when it's important. I didn't listen to Lily when she told me not to come here. that I'd look desperate or something. why do I have to think I know everything? why do I . . .

–*Hey baby. You're lookin' fine.*–

–*Huh?*– I don't recognize the voice. I don't know what it said. I turn around. rattled. like I was just awakened from sleeping or something. He's up real close. right behind me. I see his eyes first. those red eyes. they're hard to miss. I guess he thinks he's being cute or something. Something else I might've missed.

–*Hey! Snap out of it, Chan. What's wrong with you anyway? You look like a little bird. like BOO! and you'll fly away.*– I don't know what's wrong. what's come over me. Marc's laughing. I'm coming around, though. getting over it. I'm smiling once I'm used to it. used to the sight of his face. of who he is and figuring out where I am. Strange moments like that make me afraid. moments when you forget everything you've ever known about yourself. your life. about anything at all. especially when there's nothing to cause it. it freaks me out a little bit.

–*Where's Jay? You've seen him?*–

–*Yeah, he was just here. He'll be back. Why? something wrong? you're lookin' like a ghost, babe.*–

–*No. it's nothing. I was just wondering if you'd seen him is all. I'm fine.*–

–*Alright then, if you say so. like I said, he'll be right back.*– Marc starts walking away. He looks hurt. I guess I was kind of blowing him off. I stop him. I didn't mean to be mean. just pulling myself together you know.

I run the few steps to get next to him. I put my arm around him. He looks a little shocked. I've never done this to him before. I don't care, I'm in a good mood again. slowly. still scared the way my mood comes and goes. how quickly it's coming back. or else I just want to pretend. like nothing bothers me ever. that nothing's ever wrong. that I'm in a good mood but it may be that I'm just pretending.

There's a bunch of kids around. I don't know them. don't really want to. college kids. fucking rejects. I don't want to get personal with any of them. It'll just make me mad. I don't want to know any real people. just us. the trash. these kids don't look at me like that because they're too cool for it. but they think it. deep down they do. Marc could care less. he's just hanging out with them. taking whatever he can get from them.

I stay to the outside. not making eye contact but smiling like I have a secret they all want to know. The guys are look-ing at me. all of them. like a little pack of perverts in heat. because I'm young. because my shirt's too small. because they can see my underwear. because it's my beautiful night. but it's not for them. when I put my hand up to my mouth, that's not for them. look but don't touch. it's not for you. when I open my mouth, that's not for them. when I lift my arms in the air. waving. yelling. that's not for them. It's for him. for Jay. because I'm so happy once I see him. for real, finally. finally see him walking down the street, toward us, and I'm happy even though he doesn't even see me. I'm happy.

*   *   *

He's holding my hand when we walk through the doors. it's sweaty. it's not gross, it's cute. I like it. The stairs stretch out in front of us. the walls are so red. like lipstick. it's dark. I hope it's dark enough so that he can't see me shaking. I'm still a little on edge, but I'm happy too. it's confusing. I'm smiling. but I don't want him to see me.

There's no one in front of us. no one behind us. the stairs climbing in front of us. my hair looks so yellow in this new light. like a dream or something.

It's not as loud as I thought it would be. as loud as I knew it was going to be. The band isn't playing yet. just the stereo. or someone playing records or something. same thing. I don't see them at first. looking over here and over there. then I see them. Over there in the corner. Lily's dancing. she looks crazy. jumping around.

Elizabeth sees me. she's running up to me. she's so happy. I can see it in her eyes. can see it because of the way my reflection looks in her eyes. it's all of a sudden the way it hits me. the way I realize that the last two hours is the most I've been away from her. the longest she's been out of my sight since the last time. the night of that party. I know by the way she's holding on to my hands. trying to get me to dance. I can't believe I didn't realize before. I mean, how much I need her. maybe that's why I've been so on edge. so crazy. so confused. so nervous, I guess. it's because she needs me. and I need that. it's like part of me is missing when she's not there. it was hard to see it. but now it's so clear. now that she's holding my hands. smiling.

–I missed you– she whispers. It's too loud to hear her, anyway.

People are bouncing by us. spilling drinks. singing. They are older people. mostly 18 or older because that's what the flyer says: **18 and Over.** This one girl brushes beside me. Bumps into Elizabeth. The girl's bag hits Elizabeth right in her face. Elizabeth shakes it off. She's just happy to be here. But I'm pissed. I want to say something when the girl turns around and apologizes to me. She doesn't even see Elizabeth!

I don't understand. Then I look around. I notice it. how small she is in this room of college kids and adults. 11 years old! 11 years old? She should be riding bikes. should be drawing rainbows and reading stupid books about streetkids. She shouldn't be here. the pounding music. the angry smell of alcohol. the people with all their adult problems and adult stuff. But she's happy. So fucking happy. Holding my hands, her clean blue eyes staring at me. so warm. so friendly. She should be in the suburbs somewhere with friends, sitting on the green, green lawn like commercials for insurance or something. talking about boys for the first time. eating dinner with a mom and with a dad that love her.

But then I remember her dad. how I said I would kill him if he ever showed up, and I think . . . maybe she's better off. here. with me. 11 or not, she belongs here. We both do.

I saw Jef today. Jef, my former brother. my former guardian and former best friend. I don't see him so much anymore. He looked pretty bad. thin. It was good to see him anyway. I miss seeing him. even if he's not the same. so thin. Ever since he and Ty. I don't know. once they started getting high together. well. I just don't see him much is all. I don't care really. it's just that I wish I saw him more.

I remember how we used to always be together. like never apart for anything. kind of like me and Elizabeth are now, I guess. I remember one time waking up next to him. it was dark. I could still make out his face even though it was dark. I knew it by heart. like I'd always known it. he was perfect. I don't see that face. not today. it's there, but it's faded. I miss that Jef. the one that was like my brother. I miss how he used to take care of me like I take care of Elizabeth.

He won't look at me. looks at the ground. at the sky. looks everywhere but he won't look at me.

I don't recognize his voice. it's so thin. like a ghost's. It's like he doesn't even know me. when I jump into his lap, he looks so startled. it scares me. I move. sit next to him on the bench. I try to get him to look at the roofs of the buildings. to see the dawn like we used to. to get him to tease me. something. anything. but it doesn't get through. he's somewhere else. it's not him. not Jef. not my Jef anyway.

I don't think he comes out much. I wish I'd never left him. like it's my fault or something. like caring for me gave him a reason to keep clean. I'm sorry. DO YOU HEAR ME? I'm sorry. I'll come back. I'll do anything if you'll put your arm around me again. talk to me in a voice I know again.

He'll be okay, though. maybe tomorrow. maybe the next day. but he'll be okay again soon. I know he will. He has to be. –*Chan?*– and it's like it's the first time he notices that I'm sitting there. that I've been next to him for the last twenty minutes. It's not his voice, though. someone else's. like it's going to break. shatter at any moment. at the next syllable. I want him to stop speaking. I don't want him to talk. not in that voice. not in the ghost's voice. if he's going to talk to me, I want it to be him. I want it to be Jef. the boy who looked after me. the one who took care of me. that's

94

who I want talking to me. not this person that's here. next to me. it's not him.

–*Chan?*– I'm crying now. tears at the corners of my eyes and I'm afraid if he says my name again that they're going to fall. that I'm not going to be able to help it. –*Look, do you have any money? Can I borrow a couple of dollars or something? I'll pay you back. promise.*–

It's hard to see. everything looks like it does when it's raining. It's hard to breathe, but I take the money out of my pockets. I don't want it back. I don't even care. I don't want to give it to him. I know I might never see him again. $7. that's all I have. all I'm worth to him now.

–*Thanks.*–

He doesn't look at me. I don't want him to anymore. I'm crying. I can't bring myself to say anything. –*Umm hmm*– is all I can get out. He doesn't even say goodbye. I don't want him to. I can't watch him walking off. I think I'm going to pass out. it's so hard to breathe.

and he's gone. just like that. disappears. lost in the faces of all the people I never knew and never will. never want to.

–Was that Jef? Where's he going?–

I lift my face from my hands. tears all down my cheeks. my palms. my eyes are swollen. I can't breathe. can't say anything. Elizabeth stands there. staring at me. the sun behind her. I can barely see her. I don't want her to fade away. I'm scared of her fading away. washing away like side-walk drawings. the tears in my eyes making it hard to think of anything else.

I hold my arms out for her. I'm crying so hard. She doesn't say anything. doesn't need to. I hold on to her. so tight. I've never needed her more than I do right then. never needed anyone like that. I'm so relieved she doesn't ask me what's wrong. I couldn't bear that right now. I think she knows. or at least she knows I don't want to talk about it. I just want to cry. want her hands on the back of my head. Let me cry. please. not too long. let it all be okay. I want everything to be okay.

I must have fallen asleep or something. the sun was so warm. it's easy to fall asleep then. I kept my eyes closed. I wanted to hear the sounds of the city and picture it all. the cars. the summer breezes blowing through the trees and the shade passing in and out above me so that my eyelids go dark and then bright red.

I hear kids playing in Spanish. I don't want to open my eyes. I want to watch them run around in my head. chasing each other. the short, quick screams. the kind of happy screams that kids make. on swings. running back and forth and everything.

There's a pigeon. it's very close to me. I'm listening to it. coming closer. it must be right next to my head. I'm trying not to giggle. I don't want to scare it away. it's purring so loud. I won't open my eyes. trying to picture it. once I've got it for certain in my head, then I'll open my eyes. if only to see how right I am. I almost laugh. I think it's going to step on me soon. I imagine it must be beautiful. it's mostly white. except for the neck. the neck is green and purple. iridescent. like stars. those dark eyes. secret eyes.

It's the patter of little shoes that does it. makes it fly away. makes me open my eyes. a little boy. the little brute. I smile at him. He has his hands above his head like a monster. a pigeon monster. running on to the next crowd of birds. I watch them fly away. I never see the one. It will always be the way I imagined it.

Rubbing the glare out of my eyes. the sun shines right on me. I sit up. half asleep. half tired. The police cars are lined up on the other side of the street. parked in front of the station. it's a pretty station. even if the police are ugly, I like the building anyway. even the way the sun shines on the cars is almost pretty. the blue numbers. the sirens.

I hear her, but I don't see her. she was right here next to me before I fell asleep. she's on the other side of the fence. in the playground. I watch her. she doesn't know I'm watching. it's my secret. she's playing with the Spanish kids. she doesn't know what they're saying. she doesn't care. neither do they.

They run around in circles. I can't figure out what game they're playing. one of those little kid games. the kind that don't have any rules. or rules you make up as you go along. just a lot of running around. a lot of laughing. Elizabeth's older than the rest of them. they all gather around her. look to her to make up the rules.

I watch her. out of breath. glowing. sweat on her forehead. She has my shirt on. the one with the daisy. the one I gave to her. must have been two months ago. I want so much for her. want her to have a normal life. I imagine how she must've looked when she was real young. in the schoolyard. two braids like always. she deserves that kind of life. a real life. one you see on television every day. it's not for me, but it's right for her. fits her.

She's in charge out there. on the playground. That's how I know. That's how I know she was happy in her old life. I don't mean at her house. I mean, that's how I know everyone must have liked her at school and things. She stands with all those little kids around her, running around her and hanging on every word she says though they don't understand a lot of it.

I can see her, if I look the right way, I can see her running in from recess. Can almost picture it perfectly. I can see the other girls following her because she is the nicest one. because they trust her. I can see her like the teacher must have seen her, sitting in the classroom and watching as the students run in. Elizabeth in front. her cheeks glowing and her eyes. The sunlight shining off them like expensive glass. teacher's pet kind of eyes. Then I think about the teacher. How could they have let her run away? Why didn't they protect her?

I come around the gate. She doesn't see me at first. She's bending down. saying something to one of the children. I don't move. I'm afraid if I do I will ruin the whole thing. I just stand. I will wait until she sees me. sees me watching her. watch as they all start running around again. screaming. happy screams.

Her hand shoots up in the air. it's so small. waving back and forth. I take a few steps. don't want to go all the way over there. don't want to spoil the game. the sun is so warm shining down on me. holding my arms behind my back.

–*Hi!*– she's out of breath. wiping the sweat off her forehead. –*I was just fooling around. You fall asleep?*– I nod. I'm smiling so hard. squinting. –*You wanna go? We can.*– I don't say anything. Three little kids run up and grab on to her. they answer her question, pulling her away. they want her to play some more. they're not finished playing. the game's not over. I watch her go. watch her play. I never want to stop her. just let her go forever. running. happy. alive like she was always meant to be.

It's been kind of weird around this place the last couple of days. the way Lily and Eric have been arguing. It's too much like a real home now. too real. They don't speak to each other much. When they do, I don't want to be around. it's bad. they start yelling. calling each other names and everything. I hate it. I wish they'd just be happy, but I guess it's too late for that. I don't really want either of them to leave, but I think it's going to come to that. I don't know which one I want to stay. I mean, Lily's my friend. she's a girl and all. But without Eric here, we might all have to leave. we'd never be safe without at least one boy around. It's not that stupid stuff, you know, like all girls are weak or anything. It's just with a guy around, other guys keep their distance. It's the way things are, is all. I wouldn't *feel* safe anyway. I would have to leave and then Lily would hate me.

Lily says it's all Eric. he's being a total creep. I guess she ran into Scott the other night. he was by himself. she says nothing happened. she's lying. I was there. I saw them kissing. but it was okay. I mean, it wasn't that bad. Eric was kind of freaking out for no reason. It wasn't like he thinks it is. they're old friends. they just missed each other. it's not like they were going to get back together or anything. it was nothing really.

They're fighting right now. in the other room. Lily is yelling so loud. she's hitting him. over and over again with her fists. Elizabeth is upset. says it's too much like how her father used to fight with her mom. I tell her it's nothing like that. not to worry. but it keeps going on. every night. all night. it is like that. exactly like that. it's not fair.

Eric's trying to stay quiet. but it won't last. it's the same thing every time. He keeps it in until it just comes out. then he will be yelling too. he won't hit her, though. thank god. I wouldn't be able to handle that. he yells, though. he sounds so angry. like he's not even a person anymore. just a color or something. just a voice. a really angry voice like a big blue light shining all fierce and mean.

I want to go outside. to get out of here. just walk around. come back later. But it's late. past three in the morning. I don't care if I am a streetkid, I'm still not going out now. I'm still only 15 years old. it's not safe. Maybe if I was a boy or something. maybe if I didn't have Elizabeth to worry about too. but I'm not and I do. I'm not going out there. I'll just have to sit here. awake. listening. wishing I didn't have to.

It's Eric. he's the one who finally moves out. the one who can't take it anymore. I knew it would be. He's gone in the morning. Lily hasn't slept. She watched him leave. I feel like throwing up when I see her. She looks sick. It makes me sick. knowing I have to leave her too. That I have to move somewhere else.

She says she isn't going to go with us. that there's no reason to leave. Elizabeth is mad at me too. She doesn't want to go. doesn't see why we have to. But I think she does. otherwise she would fight me more. would be madder than she is. She knows she doesn't want to stay here without Eric any more than I do. That's not why she's mad. I know. that's why I don't give her a hard time when she gives me one.

I'm not looking forward to it. to finding a new place. This is the best place I've lived in. I should've known it couldn't last forever. I guess I did deep down. I always knew. sucks, is all. sucks for all of us. me. Elizabeth. Lily. even Eric. he was happy here too.

Lily won't even look at me. She sits there. facing the corner. nothing on the floor. *–Lily, you know it's the right thing to do–* I say. I want to leave. I've had enough trying to talk to her. But I'm scared. afraid to just leave her here. *–Please! You know there will be 10 dirty creeps in here soon and I don't want to be around when they get here.–*

–Go on then! No one's stopping you. Get the FUCK out!–

I can still hear her yelling at me. at the bottom of the stairs I can still hear her. walking through the door, pulling Elizabeth with me by the hand. I can still hear her on the street. leaning out the window. screaming at me. calling me names. hating me. hating me so loud I can hear her when I turn the corner. I think I might go on hearing her my whole life. but I get far enough. I'm not certain of the exact moment, but I don't hear her anymore. maybe she just stopped yelling. maybe I just stopped listening. I'm not sure. but I'm glad I can't hear her anymore.

I don't know where to go. I don't know many people anymore. not any I can just show up and move in with. I don't want to go to Jay's. I don't want to give him the wrong idea. or worse, make him think he's got to protect me now. But there really is nowhere else. so maybe for the night. that's all we need. a place for tonight and then a place for the next and the next. I've done this before. I shouldn't be worried but I am. it never felt like this. or maybe it did. but it feels worse this time. or I just don't like the way it feels anymore. not knowing where to go. what's next. where you're going to be next week. next year.

We have enough money. we could stay in a hotel. I'd rather not. the money goes quick that way. besides, I don't want to get used to it. to a soft bed. a shower. before you know it, you won't leave. the money will be gone in a couple of weeks. then we'll be right where we started. nowhere. no hope and nothing to keep it going.

We'll find someone. somewhere. We'll wait in the park. It's the best thing really. best chance we have. there's always *someone* there. I just don't know which one. probably Washington Square. but maybe not. it's summer. lots of tourists. maybe Tompkins Square *is* better. I can't make up my mind. maybe it doesn't matter either way. but I'm mad at myself for not being able to choose. for not knowing. I have to be the one. the one who knows what's the best thing all the time. I got to. I should anyway.

Okay. we'll just go to Tompkins Square. it's closer. it's right there. that's it, it's the right one. I think. I'm not sure but I can't take being unable to make up my mind anymore. I have to convince myself. talk myself into it. that's where we're going. we're already there.

I don't want to go too far in. in case I want to leave. We are about to sit down when I see Eric. alone. I'm not sure we should go over there. but we do.

–Hey– I say softly. because I don't think I can say it any louder. because there's this terrible secret behind anything we say to each other right now. anything we say is tainted. like it's dirty. he knows it. that's why he says *hi* real quiet back to me.

–You left– he says. I nod. he knew I would. I feel so stupid. like his kid or something. like I would feel if I ever went back to my dad, I guess. Here we are, me and Elizabeth. looking at him like he just abandoned us. He didn't. I know that. Everyone out here's on their own. I *know* that. But I can't help looking at him that way. can't help feeling that way. feeling like I want him to take us back. I want to promise it will be fine if he just comes back. But it won't. I know that too.

None of us says anything but we all stand up at the same time. it just feels right. like the right time. We are going with Eric. We're going to stay with him. for tonight and that's it. maybe the next night too. but not forever. He says

106

he knows a place. it's on the Lower East Side. He says he found it last week. he always keeps his eyes open. says you never know when you'll have to find someplace else. He hopes it's still empty. says it might be. that it wasn't that nice. that it was kind of hidden.

I don't like the Lower East Side. I don't come down here much. it's ugly. the people are ugly. you know, not ugly like ugly looking, but ugly underneath. strange. weirdos. like middle aged guys with Band-Aids on every finger. old Chinese ladies with chicken bones and strange stuff like that. you know. really creepy stuff. I definitely don't want to stay down here. not long anyway. I'm not sure it's any better than staying alone. in our old place. it felt like home anyway. not like this. not like a nightmare.

The building looks like it might fall down. crash on top of us if we breathe too hard. too often. there are bricks missing in the brick wall. windowsills missing from the windows. maybe it was nice once. like a million years ago. 1936 or something. but now it's a dump. a squat. you can't get in from the front. probably why it's still empty. you have to go around to the back through a vacant lot. have to get in through the basement. I can hear the rats run when I climb through the window. when I put my feet on the cement floor. in the puddle. they run but it's me who wants to run.

The door leading into the rest of the house is locked. Eric says maybe we should stay in the basement tonight. look for something else tomorrow. Says it's probably safer anyway. he doesn't think this place is too steady. The thought of sleeping down here is worse than anything. almost anything anyway. It's not worse than thinking about going back out there. trying to find someplace else while the sun starts going down. when you start walking faster because you might not find anywhere. that's worse. worse than this, I guess. not much, but it is.

It's no use. I wake up every twenty minutes or so. thinking about Lily. how I could just leave her there. if she's even still there, that is. did I betray her? choose sides? choose Eric over her? It didn't feel like that. not at the time. I was choosing one thing over another. choosing a situation, not a person. not one person over the other. I would never do that. that's what my daddy did. chose her over me. my stepmom. I never want to be like that. never want to make that kind of choice. I didn't, though. I keep telling myself that I didn't but I'm not sure I believe myself. but I have to. I'll throw up if I don't. tear my eyes out and everything. That would mean I'm like him. like my dad. and that would kill me.

She's fine, though. Lily. I'm worried about nothing. making it up so that I can feel like she needs me or something. I know she doesn't. why should she?

It's the rats is all. the rats are what's really keeping me up. scurrying back and forth. their long tails. all naked. squeaking. splashing in the puddles on the floor. water dripping from the ceiling, leaking through the walls. there must be hundreds of them in here. I feel them brush up against me. one ran over my legs. I couldn't close my eyes after that. I imagined them all around me. too many to keep away.

Elizabeth sleeps the entire time. I don't want to wake her up. That's too selfish. I want to talk to her. to not be alone. but not that way. not by making her feel the way I feel. that's not what I want. I let her sleep. I can handle it.

Maybe if I think about something else. maybe that will do it. maybe if I think about somewhere far away. somewhere just for us. like where we will go once we leave. I've never been able to see it before. too afraid to. but now I'm too afraid not to. I see Elizabeth. she's climbing the side of a small house. a ladder leaning against it. there's flowers in a garden below her. I see her seeing me. I've never seen her so happy. her hair is like black sunshine. I'm standing below her. trees all around me. lots of trees. tall. lots of leaves. colors like crayons. everything's so pretty. so warm. like heaven on the tv. a happy ending. It's pretty to think so. to forget how ugly and dirty we are. here. with the rats everywhere.

We went to Jay's early. for a visit. I wanted to dig myself out of that basement as soon as I could. get away from the rats.

–*You're lucky they ain't come and bite your noses off. pretty little noses that they are.*– Jay's trying to cheer us up. playing around. –*They're known to do that, you know? Just come right up to you and all.*– He pins my arms to my side. I can't move. he's on top of me pretending to bite off my nose. I'm laughing so hard. I laugh harder when he misses. when he actually bites me by accident.

and I'm glad he's who he is. glad he knows how to make me feel better. I need that. after spending the night in the worst dump in my life, I need that. but I want him to stop. I fight him off. Scott showed up a few minutes ago and I don't want to talk about it with him here.

–*Stop it!*– I finally have to say because Jay won't get off me. won't let my hands free so that I can stop laughing. He doesn't get off, but he does stop. sitting in my lap. he's small for a guy. my size. I like that. I like him sitting in my lap.

–So. I don't get why you guys didn't just stay here after the whole Eric and Lily thing.– well, that's that I guess. we're going to have to talk about it now. but I only get a little mad. It's not Jay's fault. I didn't say anything to him like *–don't say anything when Scott gets here.–* I should have but I didn't. I want to be mad at him but I can't. he's too cute. I push him off my thighs. punishment, kind of.

It only takes Scott a few seconds longer than I thought to catch on. *–What do you mean?–* he perks up. anything about Lily makes him perk up. normally it's kind of sweet but today it just makes me sad. *–Why, where did you stay last night? Did something happen to your place?–*

–Sort of– I say. *–Just that it's not our place anymore.–* I'm being kind of a bitch, I know. but that's the only way I'm going to get through this without crying. without hating him for everything that's happened.

–Yeah? why? what happened, anything?–

–Yeah, something.– the whole thing is uncomfortable. this conversation.

–Come off it, Chan. C'mon. tell me what happened.–

–What do you want me to tell you, Scott? that Lily and Eric broke up? that she was a mess? that I don't even know where she is? Is that what you want me to tell you? will that make you shut up?–

He doesn't say anything. he doesn't know what to say. no one does. Elizabeth gives me that look. the one that lets me know she's disappointed in me. I don't fucking care, it's not like I wanted to talk about it in the first place. They're all looking at me. I want them to stop. LOOK THE OTHER WAY! I want them to stop before I start crying again. they won't. they keep their eyes right on me. and I can't keep it in.

That's been happening too often lately. me crying. I never used to cry. but it's happening now and I don't know how to stop it. I feel so dumb. with everyone looking at me and everything. for what I said to Scott. It wasn't his fault. none of it was. I don't know why I said it was. or made it seem that way. he looks hurt. looking at me. I can see him. he's all blurry.

–I'm sorry. I didn't. I mean. well. I'm sorry, is all. I'm sorry.– then I really lose it. I'm sorry for everything. sorry

I snapped at him. sorry I ruined the afternoon. we were having fun. honest. I had forgotten about yesterday. almost. I wasn't thinking about it anyway. then this! and it all comes right up to the top again. the fighting and yelling. the rats running over me. not being able to sleep. being worried sick that Lily is dead or something. worried that me and Elizabeth may end up having to stay another night there.

Jay is frightened. he's just sitting there. doesn't know what to do. what to say. Why should he? he's just a boy after all. they always only know how to say the wrong things. or do the wrong things. like just sitting there. that's the wrong thing to do.

Scott. he's no use either. waiting for me to start talking again. to tell him more. why should I? what makes him think I even want to ever speak again? I can't breathe. please. one of you be sensitive. for once. please. just for one fucking minute. just until I'm okay again. is that too much? STOP staring at me! do something! PLEASE!

I feel her touch my hand. I can't look. it's cold. her hand. so soft too. fits perfectly. The look on her face is gone. the one that makes me feel so guilty. so small. it's been erased. replaced by the only one that could make me stop sobbing right now. the one that looks scared. the one that needs me. needs me to not act like this. like everything's coming apart.

I put my arms around her. leaning over. against her. Jay is still sitting there beside me. not sure what to do with himself. with his hands. he puts them in his pockets. puts them up to his face. anything but putting them on me, like I'm contagious or something. but at least he changed his expression. if nothing else.

I wipe the hair out of my eyes. my palms are all wet. snotty. but I'm okay now. I will be. as long as I don't look at either of them, I'll be okay. as long as I keep facing my lap. my hands. or the floor. anything but seeing them. seeing their eyes.

I'm going to tell them like this. while I'm not looking. It will be easier. I'll be able to get through it. I mean, it's not so much what happened that's got me so upset anyway. it was nothing really. I mean, in the scheme of things. it was other stuff. stupid stuff. stuff I don't even really have to worry about but I do.

—All of us left last night. We left Lily there. I don't know where she went. I'm sorry.—

Scott was really good. He didn't freak out or anything. I'm not sure why I thought he would. but he didn't. and he didn't ask why, if that's all that happened, why I'd gotten so weird all of a sudden. He stayed calm. real nice about it and all. –*What happened?*– that's all he asked. and that's the only thing he could've asked that wouldn't send me off to somewhere else again. somewhere I didn't want to go.

–*Her and Eric got in a fight. We left. went with him. I'm sorry.*–

–*Why are you sorry?*–

–*Don't know. I feel terrible about leaving her, I guess. I hope she's okay, is all.*–

–*She's fine. You wanna go look for her? We'll come with you.*–

–*Thanks.*– I don't think I could've gone alone. I mean, with just me and Elizabeth. not sure she wanted to see us. I wouldn't be able to handle it if she didn't want to talk to us. I wouldn't know what to say by myself either. I want to go. just not right now. I want to wait. I need to wait a little bit. I'll be ready in just a little bit. we'll go then.

*   *   *

We all go together to find her. I know we'll find her. that I'm just nervous for no reason. She's probably sitting in the bedroom right now. smiling up at the ceiling. happy as she's ever been now that she has the place to herself. I hope so.

I see Jay trying to stay as far as possible from me. he's scared of me. scared I'm going to hate his guts for being such a dork earlier. scared I don't like him anymore or something. it's cute. I should make him sweat it out. make him go on like this for days. but I can't help myself. I want to be selfish. I want to be in a good mood. it's been too long. I hate being sad and depressed.

I slow down so he doesn't see me. then I'm going to sneak up. I'm going to get right up next to him. he still doesn't notice. still just walking along. I'm like a snake. waiting to bite. to get him. waiting for the right moment. and then it comes. he stops. I feel my feet leave the ground. my arms around his shoulders. I jump on him. we both fall down. tumble onto the sidewalk. Scott and Elizabeth keep walking. smiling at each other.

I help Jay get up and we start walking. staying a little in back of Elizabeth and of Scott. *–Aren't you going to put your* *arm around me?–* I ask. teasing him. it feels good. having him smile at me again.

–I thought you hated me or something– he says.

–No.–

He has his arm around me now. we kind of stumble until we're in step. then it's easier. walking's easier. with someone helping you I mean.

–You looked at me so strange. You know?–

–Because you were being dumb. That's why– I told him.

The last thing I'm going to do is explain to him how I felt. He wouldn't understand anyway. I'm not sure he even wants to know. I just know that I don't want to talk about it anymore. I want him to hold my hand. to keep smiling at me. That's all I want right now.

I had a doll when I was little. I took her with me every-where. it didn't matter. to the store. to school. anywhere I went, she went with me. I never even named her. It's funny but I never felt the need to. I tried to once but none of the names I could think of seemed right. none seemed perfect enough. so I didn't use any of them. wasn't like she needed one. I wasn't making introductions. whatever I said to her was just to her. she didn't need a name for that.

I left her at home when I left. It wasn't a sad moment or anything. It's not like I'd even played with her for forever. I didn't even think about it at the time. but I miss that doll sometimes. miss just having her around. It taught me how to take care of things. taught me just how to hold someone that wants to be held. where to put my hands. how to listen even when nothing's being said.

I wish it had taught me how to deal with this. with Lily not being there once we get there. I mean, what do you do then? when everything you've been afraid of comes true? Scott said I shouldn't worry. that she probably just went out and is on her way back. but I know that's not true. I know because all her stuff is gone. because the mirror's broken in the bathroom. blood on the floor. on her clothes too probably if only I could see them. I can't. I can't see them because she's not here. not coming back either. and I can't learn how to deal with that from a doll that's not here.

I'm not crying. I'm not even sad. I don't know what I am, but I'm not sad. I'm not angry at myself. not anymore. I'm not scared. I'm just, I don't know. I'm just kind of nothing, you know? blank. empty inside. maybe I just did my crying earlier and now it's too late to start over. maybe part of me doesn't care at all what happened here. at least I'm not sure I want to know. so maybe. maybe I don't care.

I guess everything is clearing. like the wind blowing and any branches in the way are moved aside. The sky suddenly open and it makes you open your eyes. mine are. open, I mean. Now they are.

When I left home I thought it would be great, you know. no parents. no one looking over your shoulder and getting into everything you do. It would be like Halloween and Easter all wrapped up into one or something. I guess I didn't realize that you become your own parent pretty fast. looking over your own shoulder. questioning every little thing. everything you've ever done. everything you're going to do. like whether or not you should go here or there or not go. like whether or not I should've gone with Eric and not stayed here with Lily. those kinds of things. Sometimes it would be nice just to have someone to ask. to get advice. even if you don't listen to it. even if you still make the wrong choice, at least you asked, right? even if it's just some stupid doll that doesn't even say anything. it would just be nice, that's all.

It's raining when my dad comes into the bedroom. gray and pretty. I want to go back to sleep more than anything but I won't. not yet.

It looks like my room but it's not. has those paper doors. all Japanese and everything. I look out the window. it's set up like those houses. the ones in those movies. the ones where the voices never match up right. you know? with a courtyard in the middle. not a front yard or a backyard. it's in the center instead. the house wraps around it. it's so perfect. that's how I know I'm dreaming. not then though. when I wake up.

–*I'll be back soon, princess*– my dad says to me.

He kisses me. sitting on the edge of my bed. He's someone important. I'm so proud of him. he looks so professional. he has a new suit that my mom bought him. she never died. not in my dream. not in this one. she's not there, but she is. I can see her even though she's not in the room. she's beautiful. I hold on to that image of her. hold on to it to like an old picture. hold on to it when I'm waking up. but the corners are bent. the picture's fading too. it will be gone soon, but I have it as long as I hold on really tight.

I'm not sure where I am. where it is I'm waking up. It's really dark. I can't see anything. we've been moving around so much. every day it's the same thing. I wake up. look around. have no idea where I am. the feeling doesn't last long. only a few seconds, but they go by in slow motion. Then I remember something that helps me remember more. a word or a sentence. some sequence of events. some person or something else that tells me and then I can remember. Sometimes I wonder if it would be better if I didn't remember anything at all.

Tonight it's Jay. sleeping next to me. his place. has been for the last three days. I guess I should be used to it by now. I guess it should feel like home. it will. just doesn't yet.

That night, the night Lily wasn't there, Elizabeth and I stayed. we thought maybe if we stayed, she'd come back. It was silly I guess. but we really believed it. like believing is an art. like being a little kid waiting for Santa, you know. like if you believe hard enough then whatever it is you're wishing for will come true. but that doesn't work.

Lily didn't come back. not that night and not ever. We stayed there for five nights. each night was worse than the one that came before it. I felt so lonely there. Finally we had to leave. some older homeless creeps took it over. real scary types. you know? We moved out the second they moved in. snuck out so they didn't see us.

After that we just kind of bounced around for a few days. we could've stayed with Jay the whole time. I knew that. he asked. I don't know, I just didn't feel right about it. what with Scott living there too and all. but in the end, it's the only thing that I did feel right about. I'm still not 100% certain, but I'll get used to it. I'm 100% certain that it's better than any other place we've been in.

There's a lot of people living here. too many. maybe 30 or 40. depends on the day. it makes me nervous with that many people. having all that money on me all the time. all the money we've saved. Jay doesn't know about the money. I told Elizabeth not to tell him. I just don't want him to know. not yet. I started keeping it in my underwear when I had no place to hide it. that makes me more nervous. I want to get rid of it sometimes. I want to get out of here.

I want to go back to sleep. back to the nice house that's all foreign and everything. I want to go back to my daddy. I want to hear him say my name just once. to hear his voice. to hear the rain falling in the courtyard. Maybe if I close my eyes I can make it back there. maybe if I wish hard enough. maybe. maybe then my mom won't be dead anymore and I'll never have ended up here anyway. then I think I'll live in that dream forever. the one where he loves me. where everything is perfect.

Elizabeth and I decided we deserve it. a little trip. a day off from our lives. We take the train out to Coney Island. $1.50 each way for each of us. we can afford that. don't tell anyone we're going. just go.

Lying here in the sand makes me feel like I'm real. it's so exotic. being on the beach in the middle of a city that has no nature anywhere. looking at the sun through sunglasses. I feel like I'm a million and two miles away from everything. from the dirty people I beg change from. and the traffic that passes me at all hours. I feel like someone different. someone with somewhere to go back to.

Must be 1000° today. at least that much. in the sun anyway, it's real hot in the sun. I don't mind, though. It feels good. the breeze coming off the waves in the ocean. the planes passing in the sky above our heads. I wipe my hair from my eyes. wipe the sand off my face.

–*You wanna go swimming?*– I ask. I do. the waves washing up, it looks great. the water will feel nice.

–*For real? No way!*–

–*Yeah, why not?*– who wouldn't want to? it's hot, we know we're dirty, and it's hot. I reach over to where she's lying on the blanket we brought with us. poking her in the ribs and everything. –*C'mon! c'mon!*– and she giggles like crazy. yelling at me to stop because it tickles but I'm not going to stop until she says she'll go swimming with me.

–*OKAY, FINE! just stop already*–

I stop. Elizabeth lies back down.

–Well? let's go.–

–What are we going to go swimming in anyway? I know I forgot MY bathing suit.–

–So. Who needs a bathing suit. I'll go in my underwear, what's the difference?– I take off my shirt and pants. I mean, who cares? really? looks like a bathing suit anyway. same thing.

I run down to the water. it's so cold. my feet are so cold. I have goosebumps all over my body. Elizabeth hasn't moved. A big wave splashes against my stomach. I scream. laughing.

I see Elizabeth getting up. slowly. she's so shy about getting undressed. it's kind of funny. kind of cute. like she has anything to see anyway. She walks down to the water with her hands folded in front of her chest. I'm in far enough for the water to rest on my shoulders. she turns her back to the first wave that sneaks up on her. she screams too. holds her arms out to her sides like Jesus or something. like a scarecrow. like some small, pretty, frightened bird.

I watch her. the reflection of the sun off the water. the glare of the water on her skin. I watch her walking toward me. sunshine in her smile. the sunlight dancing in her hair and she hops through the water. I let my feet sink in the soft sand. waiting. waiting for her to come to me.

I watch the planes fly by, one by one, lined up like a swarm of tiny flying ants in the sky. floating on my back. nothing but the water holding me up. I'm weightless. I can't hear anything but the sounds from under the water. dark sounds. I wonder if I can stay like this and float away. end up somewhere in South America or something. follow the clouds. studying them for shapes of things I know.

I don't hear her. it's weird, but I can sense her. like something in the current or something. I can feel her swimming under the water. coming toward me. like a mermaid. I don't move. I know I should, but I don't. I know she's going to do something to me. splash me. pull me under the water. something. I know. but I'm frozen. I can't move. like I'm hypnotized by whatever it is that lets me know she's coming in the first place.

Elizabeth springs through the surface like some sort of half girl, half dolphin. her whole body's almost completely out of the water, only to land on my stomach, pushing me totally under.

I stay underwater. not breathing. opening my eyes, see-ing billions of tiny bubbles grabbing for the top. seeing her short legs kicking. the way her spine curves to push her head back into the sun. I stay only a second or two longer. only long enough to see the last bubble disappear, the sand settle, and everything becoming suddenly calm.

the beach seems so far away when I open my eyes again. we've drifted pretty far out. no one near us. the ocean is all ours. no one else's. the beach 50 yards away from us. but seems farther. farther than outer space.

Elizabeth is smiling. happy with herself. I'm staring at the drops of water on her lips. the way the sun is resting so perfect on her. and I don't know what makes me do it. don't understand the feeling but I don't think there is any way to stop it. it seems so right. when I kiss her. seems so natural. I mean it isn't anything sexual. nothing gross about it. it's just, I don't know. it's just nice, is all. like sisters. something I needed to do right there. right then. and then it passed.

Elizabeth never mentions it. she never speaks about it. not when it happens. not when we get back to our blanket to dry off. not ever. I don't either. she's a little startled. a lit-tle nervous maybe. but not mad. she understands. she smiles. we swim back together. there's nothing weird about it. it's like it never happened. like our own secret. forgotten the moment it was over. maybe it was the happiest moment of our lives. maybe because we know it would never happen again. that kind of friendship. not between us. not with anyone else either.

My skin feels so warm. warm to the touch of my palm. Almost dry. It's like I can feel the sun in my hand. hold it. keep it until I open my fingers and let it fly back up into the sky. and it's already there when I open my eyes.

The sand has gotten all over the blanket. it itches. I try to brush it off. wiping it off my legs. my arms. off the blanket, but Elizabeth won't move so I can't do a good job. she's asleep. her hair is still wet. but her clothes are dry.

The beach has pretty much emptied out. all the families have gone home. I only see a few people. here and there. scattered like we were all dropped from a plane. dropped and stayed right where we landed. except the one guy. he's standing near us. looking at us through his camera. trying to find out how he can trap us forever in there. print us out like wallpaper whenever he wants.

128

–Hey! What do you think you're doing?–

I hear the tiny click of the camera's lens. I imagine myself as a photograph. the sky is grainy. faded. my eyes are hidden behind the messy strands of my hair. I can see my ribs. the bones in my back. the color of my underwear fading into the background. fading into the color of my skin. maybe I'm frowning. maybe not. depends on the exact second. I'm sure I wasn't smiling, though. I've never smiled in any picture ever taken of me.

–What do you think you're doing anyway?–

He notices me for the first time. I mean ME. the me that talks, that moves and has thoughts. that me. not the me he wanted in his pictures. not the me he made up so he could keep me forever. keep me for himself like however he wants me to be. not that person. now he is seeing me. for the first time.

He's a little startled. I can see his face when he puts the camera down at his side. hanging on a strap around his neck. he looks surprised to see I'm here. that I'm not only something he could see through his viewfinder. he looks embarrassed. kind of shy. I like that. he seems normal. not like some creep. he seems special. like an artist or something.

–What, you wanna take our picture?–

He doesn't say anything. I don't mind really. I probably sounded like I minded, but I don't. *–Well? If you wanna, you can. Just it would be nice to ask first.–*

I know I probably should have told him to piss off or something. but I don't know. It feels kinda nice. you know? to have someone pay attention to you. to look at you like that. like you are the most beautiful thing they've ever seen.

His voice is far away. the wind blowing against it. fighting it. but I hear him. *–Can I?–* he asks. it doesn't really sound like a question. more like an answer.

–Sure– I yell so he can hear me. I say it as he lifts his camera up and I hear it click, click, clicking over and over. *–For five dollars you can!–* and I hear him laughing. hear the camera again.

I don't move around much. just kind of stay there. looking at him. didn't think I gave him much to take pictures of but he keeps taking more and more. when he's done, he comes over. holding out a twenty dollar bill and a piece of paper.

–You drive a hard bargain. Here's my business card in case you find yourself needing another $5.– He's laughing. I don't think he's laughing at me, but I can't tell. I'm studying the name on the card. the way it is written. the way the letters look typed there against the white paper.

–You're really pretty, you know.– I thank him. holding the hair out of my face. There is something about him. something nice. I mean, it's not what you think. he isn't a weirdo or anything. I swear. He tells me he sometimes works for an agency. mostly commercials and stuff. advertising. could probably get me a modeling job if I'm interested. I'm excited. even if he is lying. even if I know I will never actually go. It's just exciting that he thinks I could. if I wanted to.

I can see Elizabeth's eyes. hiding. watching me. trying to guess what I'm saying. what I'm doing talking to someone we don't know. not trusting. I give the guy a fake phone number. making it up from number to number. He writes it down. says he'll call me. talk to my parents and work everything out. I tell him that if he talks to my parents before I do to tell them I say hi. Then I laugh. so does he. thinking I made a pretty joke.

I watch him for a while. walking down the beach. stopping to take pictures of anyone who looks interesting to

131

him. anyone who fits into his camera. anyone he can keep in a little box and let out only when he wants.

I notice Elizabeth sitting up. her thin shoulders parallel to the sky. not as pale as they were this morning. Her hair not as greasy, either.

–Who was that?– she asks quietly.

–Who?–

–That guy? I don't like him.–

I smile at her, at the way she is frowning. the way she is covering her flat chest with her arms because she is embarrassed. *–He's no one–* I tell her. *–just some photographer who thought we were models.–*

–Well, I still don't like him– she says. Her upper lip pouting. *–I don't like having my picture taken.–*

She's upset. I can tell. She wipes the sleep from her clean blue eyes. wipes them with the back of her hands,

132

which seem like paws. Must have gotten sand in them because her eyes get red.

–*Why not? It's fun.*– but I wish I hadn't said it as soon as the words leave my mouth. wish I hadn't said it because now I know it isn't sand that's gotten into her eyes. that it isn't just the wind blowing off the ocean that's irritated them. it's crying. Her crying, which is making her eyes red and itchy. which makes her small shoulders slump toward the ground.

I fold my knees and I'm quickly on the blanket next to her. Petting her. her hair. pulling the saltwater knots out of her hair. –*It's okay*– I say, trying to soothe her. –*I'm sorry, okay?*–

Elizabeth sniffs it all up. She's trying to be brave. –*I don't like him taking my picture*– she says and I know she isn't talking about the photographer. She doesn't tell me this. She doesn't have to. She doesn't have to tell me anything. just has to sit there. with my arm protecting her thin shoulders until the sky is gray.

It's getting late. The lights are coming to life on the boardwalk behind us. like a million electric stars. Glowing. like a million jackpots that could take our thoughts away. A million ways to have fun. A million and one gold coins falling like rain.

–Hey!– and she looks up at me. wanting to smile. wanting to not be sad anymore. to not have our day wasted. –hey, we got twenty bucks. You wanna have some fun?–

I nudge her in the arm. She's slow to smile. She's slow to say yes but eventually she does and we slip our shoes on. slip on our shirts over our heads and then we are racing. up to the boardwalk. –Last one there is a rotten egg– and I'm out of breath. Letting her win in the final stretch. Letting her smile more as we slip away into the crowd. into the thick smell of candy and bubble gum.

We're tired. after winning some games. losing some. after watching the city rise and set from the ferris wheel. after stuffing our faces with all kinds of really bad, really good food. after all of that, we're tired.

Keeping my eyes on the cracks between the wood, I walk. keep walking. watching my feet step over each one. seeing Elizabeth's tiny hands sway in and out of view. –Don't step on the crack, you'll break your mother's back– I'm whispering over and over. saying it to myself really.

don't even know I'm saying it out loud. thought I said it in my head until Elizabeth joins in.

We start singing it as loud as we can. skipping. holding hands. acting like little kids acting up or something. I don't even care about the way people are looking at us. I stick my tongue out at them. then laugh. laugh so hard it's hard to keep paying attention and I'm stepping on every crack. stepping on them on purpose. like I used to do when I was mad at my mom.

Neither of us is ready to leave. to get back on the train and head home. as if it really were a home at all. I don't think I ever wished I had a home more than I do right then. it just seems like that's where we are supposed to go. after having so much fun. like everyone else who's here. everyone else who was on the beach today. they all went home. when you don't have one, I guess you're not in such a hurry to go.

I watch the people walk by as we sit down. watch them pass like people in a parade. walking. watching the lights blinking on and off, decorating the amusement park like a Christmas tree.

–You know? We can make it out of here soon.–

135

Elizabeth doesn't look at me. keeps her eyes on her feet. she is kicking them back and forth, watching them dance. *–Okay.–* her hands are folded in her lap. *–I'm ready to go when you are.–*

–I don't mean here, here. I mean, well, I mean we can go away. Far away.–

–Where?–

She sounds scared. small. her voice is small.

–Well, I guess we can go anywhere. Why? Where do you want to go?– Truth is, I don't know where. hope she might know. because no matter how much I've been thinking about it, I always come up with nothing. I thought we could go to another city. in another state. or another country even. but then I think what's the difference. what would be the point.

She keeps her head down. keeps her hands folded. her hair hanging to cover her face. her eyes. so that I can't really see what she's thinking. *–I don't know–* she says. I guess I don't really expect her to. *–Why do we have to go anywhere?–*

136

–Because.–

–Because why? It's not so bad. I like it here.–

You won't! I want to yell. You won't next year. or next week even. you won't when it starts to seem so crowded you find it hard to breathe. you won't. the first time you start seeing the same people with their hands out every day, you won't. not when you realize they see you too. you won't then. not the first time you see one of your friends and don't recognize them because they've become so thin. so worn. when you're sick of seeing your own reflection in shop windows. dirty. skinny. ugly. you won't then. I don't want her to ever get there. to see those things. I guess I want her to always want to stay in a way. to think it's not so bad. that means she will never be where I am. at the point where she knows how bad it really is. that's why I have to get her away.

–It's better somewhere else. I promise, it's better.–

–Where else?–

–I don't know. but we'll find it. okay? you and me. we'll find it. okay?–

—okay.— and she looks at me. smiling. but softly. quietly.

We don't say anything more about it. but she knows. knows we'll be leaving soon. I want her to be ready is all. I want her to be prepared.

After a few minutes we get up. We go silently past the booths that shower us with fancy stuff to buy. to win. past the lights that reach all the way up to the sky and I can see the electricity bounce off the clouds and come back down like rain. past the houses off the boardwalk where the downstairs lights trade places with those upstairs and people are getting ready to go to bed or go out for the first time. past the cars parked up and down every street. past the people standing on the corner and we climb down the stairs to wait for the train. wait to go back into the city. back to our lives. at least for a little while. at least until we're both ready to leave. to leave it forever.

I've hidden the money. someplace secret. in the hole inside the sofa that Elizabeth and I use for a bed. The hole the roaches come out of. I hid it because I didn't want to carry it around anymore. I knew something like this was going to happen. I didn't want to have the money on me when it did. when Jay tries to take off my clothes. he's not real good at it, though. I don't mind. too nervous to mind.

He says he loves me. I believe him. says it as he's kissing me. kissing my mouth. the palms of my hands. I laugh when he does that. it tickles. I laugh when he tries to put his tongue in my mouth. it feels strange. Stranger than normal. More eager. Hungrier, kind of.

I feel a little bit like I'm drowning. covered over. but it's not a bad feeling. My heart's racing so fast I'm sure he can feel it through my chest. I don't take my eyes off his hands. moving along my ribs. down my side and over my waist. His hands are sweaty. sticking to my skin a little. I take short quick breaths. breaths like the way his hands move. stopping and starting.

It's like the darkness before a movie. like the smell of something before a fire. you know something is going to happen. know what it is too, but somehow it still surprises you.

I have my hand up to my mouth now. trying to stop my breathing. trying to stop my heart from beating so loud I imagine it can be heard from the other side of the room. My eyes are open. I don't want to close them ever again. I don't want to give in that completely.

I feel him. his hand, resting there. not knowing what to do. not sure what I want him to do. I'm not sure myself. my underwear between his hand and my skin. warm. frightened. so still. then moving so slowly it almost hurts. I don't want him to. I want it to stay still. to keep its place and hold it there forever. *—Stop.—*

Only one word. I say it so quietly I don't think I even heard it. my hand in front of my mouth and everything. my eyes still open. But he must have heard. must have, because it stops. his hand stays still for a moment, then pulls away. It's a quick movement. an angry movement. makes me wish I could take it back. the one word. but I don't want to take it back. I wanted to say it. meant to.

I reach up to touch his face. He moves away. moves off from on top of me. but doesn't move away. I feel him lying next to me. his body barely touching mine. so slightly. I don't try to put my arms around him. don't try to reach for him. waiting for him to speak. I don't say anything. waiting to hear him breathe because all I can hear is the sound of my own heart beating.

One by one I hear other sounds. sound of brakes outside the window. horns. car alarms. voices drifting up to our floor through the open window. I can hear summer dying in the wind. in leaves I didn't ever realize were there. outside our window. the open window. I can hear the stars waking up. winking. I can hear everything except Jay. I only hear silence from him.

I want to ask what's wrong, but I know the answer. besides, I don't want to be the one who talks. I don't want to hear my voice. I know it will crack if I say anything. I know it will sound fake. whatever I say.

Then I hear him. He sighs. lets out the breath he's been holding for what seems like hours, but is probably only a few seconds. My whole body jumps. I'm not expecting it. even though I am waiting for it, I don't expect it. it is so sudden. so much out of the darkness. sounds like a scream even though it's only a whisper.

I thought I was ready this time. thought I would go through with it. but I couldn't. when I felt his hand so warm, it burned. I got scared. it's not my fault. I'm not sorry for it. I'm not going to apologize again. not this time. not like the other times. I hate feeling like I should be sorry. because I do. the way he doesn't speak to me right now makes me feel that way. I hate feeling that way.

I do it. I speak first. I swore I wouldn't, but I do. I just can't stand being quiet anymore. maybe he will say something if I ask him to. *–Jay?–* I'm asking. making sure he's still right here, right now, where I am. *–Jay? say something. please say something.–*

but he only says something so wrong, it breaks my heart.

–goodnight, Chan.–

I almost think he's going to keep talking but he doesn't. hope he will tell me what he's thinking. feeling. tell me something so that I'll know if he hates me. but he doesn't say anything. his eyes are closed. I stare at them. until he turns away from me, I watch him. hoping he will do something. say something more.

The tears are hot. staining my cheeks. I'm thankful that they're silent, though. that I'm not making any sound. I don't want him to know. he doesn't deserve to see me crying. hasn't earned it. Staring at the ceiling. letting the tears come as they want. It's funny. I'm so sad. so upset. but there's something comforting about it. about the tears falling in the same path from the corners of my eyes. over my temples on each side. It will be okay in the morning. I won't hate him in the morning. he won't hate me either.

I don't know how long she's been standing there. her face peeking in the doorway. her body hugging the frame against the door. her finger in her mouth. shy. staring at me. my knees curled up. the skin against my ribs. my chest. naked. my hand covering my mouth and tears running in perfect streams down my cheeks. her eyes looking into mine. maybe she's been there the whole time. maybe she just got there. doesn't matter. she sees me. knows the whole story from one look at me.

Her eyes are like a mirror. they look just like I imagine mine to look. she doesn't know how I feel, it's impossible.

but I can't help thinking she does. that she understands. knows what I'm thinking because her eyes are exactly like mine. I need to believe she understands. need to know she'll always understand.

I smile through the tears. half smile anyway. try to. but she's gone. disappears behind the door when I smile. disappears the moment she realizes I'm watching her the same as she's watching me. and I'm all alone again. Jay next to me, but I'm all alone. smiling. crying. listening to the sounds from outside and trying to see if I can find the exact second when everything stops.

I have no idea what's going on at first. just hear the noises. the banging. like trees falling down. that is all I can think of. that trees are falling down all over the world at once. then I hear voices. familiar voices. voices of the people I live with. yelling. and voices I've never heard before. strong voices. voices telling them what to do.

The red lights are swirling around against the walls. streaming in the windows. everything looks like a spaceship or something. I can't put it all together. not right away. I think maybe I'm still dreaming. that the voices are just nightmares and the lights are just my eyes adjusting to the color.

Fire? it must be a fire. I sit right up. alert now. panicking. I shake Elizabeth's shoulder. telling her to get up. I'm glad I've been sharing a room with her again. since I stopped staying in Jay's room. glad because I probably would've died if I'd woken up and she had not been there and I thought the building was on fire and I wouldn't know if she had gotten out.

I try, but I can't smell any smoke. can't smell nothing burning. maybe I'm just too scared. not even sure if I'm breathing. awake or dreaming. but pretty sure I'm awake now. see the flashlights through the crack of the open door. hear voices closer. sound of heavy boots. close.

Elizabeth wiping sleep away from her eyes. slow at getting up. taking her time but we don't have any. I risk looking out the window. no red trucks. just a line of little white cars with flashing sirens. blue uniforms with helmets. shields. they don't have faces. or maybe I just can't see them. I can see some of the kids we live with. some of them running down the street. some of them being held. fighting to get away. some lying on the sidewalk with their hands cuffed behind their back. their faces pressed against the sidewalk.

—Jesus! Elizabeth, get up! Come on, fast!—

I'm pushing the sofa away from the wall. I slip. I'm scared. I have to move fast but I can't feel my legs. my arms. I can't think straight. pushing the couch. pulling at it, anything to get it so that I can feel my arm slide all the way up inside the hole where the money is.

It's right there. I can almost reach it. a little bit more. a little higher and I've got it. a bunch of it anyway. not sure it's all of it but it's what I can grab. I try one more time. nothing. I guess I got all of it. enough. doesn't matter, no time to check again. We have to go. I hear the door being broken open next door. Jay's room. Our room will be next.

Elizabeth takes two steps toward the door before I grab her and pull her back. almost pulling her off her feet. she grabs on to me. –Not that way!– and I guide her over to the window. to the fire escape.

I make sure she gets out first. tell her to go up. don't go to the street. they're there. waiting for us. go up. we'll be able to go down the back way. or onto the next building. or the next. anything. at least if we go up we have a chance.

The light shines on her from below. shining on her like a backlit angel in a childhood play. she stands with the city in the background like a set behind her. tiny against the buildings that reach up touching the sky. her bare feet all white. her eyes waiting for me to climb through the window. to join her. to be with her again.

Our clothes! I'm halfway outside when I remember our clothes. I don't want to leave them. two changes each. I don't want to have to get them again. don't want to give these assholes anything. I shouldn't have to. we didn't do anything wrong.

I'm so scared. I keep looking quickly to the window to make sure I can still see Elizabeth's feet. her shoes. I remember her shoes. I run to the other side of the room and get them. I run back to this side of the room and grab our clothes. my hands full of them. the beam of the flashlight hits me. feels like a bullet. I freeze. I can't move. but only for a split second. only long enough to see the second one coming up behind the first one.

I'm at the window. throwing the clothes into Elizabeth's arms. yelling at her to go. feeling them growling against the back of my neck. I can't hear what they're saying. can't hear words, just noises. I scream when the hand wraps around my ankle. looking over my shoulder. I can't see their faces. only the glare of the lights shining up from outside, bouncing off their face shields. struggling, I kick as hard as I can. watching his head snap back at the neck. I kick again. I may be small, but I know it hurt. I know because the hand let go of my foot and I slither through the window.

my hand on Elizabeth's back, pushing her up. lifting her when she stumbles. the cop leaning halfway out the window. lurking. distracting me so that I forget to keep moving.

staying still. but then I'm climbing again. watching his arms slink back in like a snake falling back into its hole.

I see flashlights dancing in every window. moving across the glass like insects. I hear something shatter way down on the street. someone threw a rock at one of the police cars. the glass lying in the front seat, I can see the pieces twinkling like stars from the roof. from the sirens flashing down on them.

I keep spinning around in circles. turning this way and that way because I don't know which way to go. I feel like one of those girls I've seen on the tv. one of those girls that's standing in the middle of the street while helicopters are blowing up things all around her. I don't want to look down the fire escape in the back. it's not going to be any better. I'm afraid. afraid to look and they see me and decide to climb up here after me sooner than they already will.

yes. it's the only choice. the other building would have to be better. the next roof over. we climb over the little wall that divides the two. run over to the door. check it just in case. just maybe it's open. but it's not. we start for the fire escape first. change our minds. climb over the next wall. and the next. three buildings away. we check the door. it's locked. we crouch down against the wall. hoping. praying they won't check this far away.

I hear them on our roof. –*Yeah, two of them*– and it sounds more like a recording than a real person. –*No, no. Girls. Two little girls.*– I look at Elizabeth, holding my finger in front of my mouth so that she knows to keep quiet. to hold her breath. she's shivering. it's not cold, but she's freezing. I hold her hand. it's so cold. we're both so quiet I'm sure the police will hear our hearts beating. so fast like tiny birds.

From one building to the next, I hear them. hear their feet pounding in my head. We can't let them catch us. I won't let them. If they catch us we're done. they'll find our parents. make us go home. make Elizabeth go home. I won't let them. I hold her hand so tight. I'm praying.

I'm watching. the puddle getting bigger. she knows I see, but I shake my head. it's not important. keeping my finger to my mouth. don't say anything. don't worry. they're on the next roof. the flashlights gliding right above our heads. the pee stain getting wider over her pants. spreading. but it doesn't matter. no one will ever know because I hear the footsteps getting farther. going back the other way. giving up. counting us among their losses.

I pull her head onto my shoulder. my hand holding the hair out of her face. my other hand still on my lips. frozen there. –*shhhh, shhhh.*– I can't stop. I promise her it's okay. maybe I'm lying, but I have to promise. have to say it just so I'll believe it. say it so my heart will stop exploding. so hers will too.

She is still shivering. crying. not making any noise. she won't until the morning. I'm not going to hear anything from her until I see the sun. until the birds speak first at dawn. That's okay. I don't want her to speak. I don't know what to say if she does. it's better this way. quiet. her head leaning on me. watching the city as it sleeps. listening for the hour when the police cars all drive away. when the voices stop yelling. We'll just rest here until then. curled up and safe.

–*shhhh, shhhh*– until she falls asleep. until then.

Elizabeth doesn't want to. never wants to look at it again, but I do. I have to. just want to walk by the front of the building one more time. to say goodbye. When I left home, I never turned around. never said goodbye to my house. I never felt right about that. I mean, the house never did anything. I wasn't running away from it. I think I hurt its feelings. I always regretted it. Since then, I've made myself promise that I would always say goodbye to any place I ever left.

The cops aren't there anymore. I didn't think they would be, but I wasn't sure. maybe just one. watching out in case any of us kids came back.

It has only been a few hours, but looking at the building now, the next morning, it feels like two hundred years have passed. It has been robbed of being a home and it has died a sudden death. it isn't fair. not to the building and not to us.

The windows on the first floor are now boarded up. the front door too. There's a notice posted to it. CON-

DEMNED BY ORDER OF THE NEW YORK CITY POLICE DEPT. for reasons it lists in such tiny print no one would ever bother to stop and read it. no one would care. It makes me angry and sad at the same time like them mixing up in my stomach all together and everything. *–It didn't do anything–* I say. Why don't they just come out and say it, that they hate it. like the house is a defect or something. *–It never did anything wrong!–*

Elizabeth just stares at me. frowning. I don't think she knows what I'm talking about. but I do. I mean, why do they have to punish the building? why do they have to mark it? why do they have to tear it down just because no one lives there? I mean, no real people anyway. We did. We lived there. I guess that doesn't count, though. not to them.

Elizabeth grabs my hand. I shake hers away, not even thinking. I don't want to be touched. too angry. I shake her hand away but I don't mean to. I'm sorry. I see her drop some of the clothes she's holding. her arms, full. I look at her. *–I'm sorry–* I say. then I let her hold my hand. I help her pick up what she dropped. I look at her so hard I think I might see through to her bones if I keep looking. I see the dirt where it's been washed away by her crying last night. see the dirt on her fingers. beneath her fingernails. on her feet and ankles where she still doesn't have her shoes on.

I forget about the house then. It isn't as important as taking care of her. making sure she gets clean. wash her clothes. make her feel better. feel real again. that's what is important right now. not saying goodbye to something that doesn't even know I've ever been there.

I find out from Eric that Jay got picked up last night. I'm pretty upset when I find out. Eric heard it from Eva who had heard it from Scott. *–Scott! Where's Scott?–* I ask. Eric says he doesn't know for sure, but he had been at Eva's earlier.

–Look, Chan, don't go over there now. Do yourself a favor. Just take a break, alright?–

I guess he's right, but I can't stop thinking about Jay. about what might have happened to him. wondering if I'll ever see him again, you know? if he's been sent home or something. Eric says not to worry about it. they don't do that so much with boys. It's mostly just with girls that they

154

try to track down the parents. you know, looking out for them. I guess they figure a boy can handle himself but that we are helpless. goes to show what they know, I guess.

I can't sit still. Can't relax. Not here. not back here in this stinky, maggot-trap basement that Eric calls a place to sleep. more like a place to get sick in. just puke your brains out in. I mean, sure. It's better than it used to be. better than that night we stayed here way back a few weeks ago. but not much. not by a whole lot that I would walk in and say –*Wow! I love what you've done to the place*– or anything like that. still rats. still roaches running around when I'm trying to sit and think and figure things out.

I'm so tired, but I wouldn't even dream about sleeping. I have to get out. go somewhere. do something. I want to go to the police station. to get Jay back. Even if he's been an asshole lately. Even if we haven't been on the best terms since I moved out of his room to sleep with Elizabeth again. Even so, I don't like thinking about him being there.

I wonder if they have him in a cell like some dirty criminal or if they are being nice to him. if he's scared or laughing. I can't decide how I want to imagine him. how I'm going to picture him sitting there. if he's pretty there with all the ugly people around or if he is one of the ugly people that just mixes in and gets lost in the scenery.

–Eric, can't we do something? I mean, can't we go there and say he's your brother or something? that you're here to pick him up?–

–No. we can't, alright? we can't do anything, so just stop talking about it for fuck's sake!–

I stick my tongue out at him.

Fine! We'll just let him rot in there. fine. I won't say anything anymore. but I want to see Scott then. I want to see someone. anyone.

I hate not having control over anything because it makes me feel small. like a little girl. Like when I still lived at home and couldn't do anything to make my mom stop dying. only sit and watch, and be good and quiet so I wouldn't upset my dad or my mom. I hate it.

I have to move around because I'm thinking about him, about my dad, when I should be thinking about Jay. I have to move around because my stomach hurts. all wrapped up

on itself. So I pace. back and forth through the dark basement while Eric tries to ignore me.

–*C'mon. let's go!*– I say to Elizabeth. She doesn't move,
though. doesn't want to leave. but I do. I have to. I don't
look at Eric, but she does. she's looking at him like she
wants him to talk to me but I don't want to talk to him. I
guess I don't really blame her. I'm acting like a crazy person, I know that. it's just. I don't know. it's just I feel like I'm
going to explode into six million tiny little pieces if I don't
get out of here. out of this place. trapped underground like
a caged animal or something. I swear I'll just explode.

–*Chan, come off it.*–

–*I'm not talking to you!*– Jerk. I turn my back on him.
don't want to see his stupid face. just because he can do it.
forget about people I mean. just because he can forget
about anyone right away like he forgot about Lily, doesn't
mean I will. I won't.

But I won't leave Elizabeth here either.

So I stand there. in the middle of the room. standing
there. not looking at either one of them.

–*Look, I'm sorry. I know this sucks. but. you know? there's not much you can do.*– He has his arm around me. I shake it off, but he puts it right back. I don't shake it off again. not sure I want to. I guess deep down I know he's right. I know it's better to just wait it out. doesn't make me happy about it. doesn't make me feel any better.

I'll just sit here in the corner for the rest of the day. sulking. if I can't do anything, can't go anywhere, then I'm not. not going to do *any*thing. not going to talk. not going to eat or sleep. not going to move a single muscle. just sit here. waiting. not thinking. not about Jay or my dad. not about me, not about anything.

I'm flying. the water is so far below me. I'm afraid of falling. I would drown. so much water. my wings wouldn't help me get out from under all that water. if I fall. the water circling over my head, getting higher and higher until it's so dark I don't notice it anymore.

I'm so tired, so weak. so afraid because all I can see is ocean beneath me. both in front of me and behind me. nothing but big blue water colored in by the sun shining. I flap my wings faster now that I'm afraid of falling. pretty, transparent, angelwings. I beat them so hard I'm afraid they may break, or just fall off because I don't know how they got there. don't know how secure they are.

I hope I have enough strength. enough energy in me to get somewhere where I can rest. but I don't see anything. only birds trying to stay clear of me. only the shortest glimpse of the fish that swim close to the surface as they glide under the water. the sun so bright in the sky that it's hard for me to see. and I keep flying straight ahead, hoping I will get somewhere eventually.

I wish I knew where I left from. where I started this. I could go back there if I did. but maybe I just started here. in the middle. I mean, what if there is no beginning. then there's no end either, right? I'm certain to drown if that's true.

I have to try to enjoy it. to be happy. to fly. but it's so much work. I'm so tired and it's harder now. harder than it's ever been. maybe I should just swim for a bit. maybe I will be able to float. just to rest. but I can't let my wings get wet. they will never dry and I will never be able to fly again. so I keep going. straight ahead.

I try, but the clouds can move faster than me. I can't get ahead of them. so many of them. dark ones. moving together, colliding. I try once to fly through them. over them. to get higher than they are because I know a storm is coming. but the clouds climb faster than me. the sky is so endless, there's no way for me to win. so I fly straight again.

The birds are coming at me now. hundreds of them. circling around me and one by one they launch right for me. screaming bird screams. I push them away one by one. but it's no use. too many of them. I didn't do anything. I don't understand why they're coming after me. I forget to fly. too busy fighting off the mean animals.

I'm falling. fast. faster than even the clouds can fall. three birds are chewing on my wings. trying to cut them off. I swing at them, but as soon as I try there's another one that's coming at my head and I have to turn back and take care of it.

it doesn't hurt. their little beaks eating through my wings like angry insects. it doesn't hurt too much when they finally get all the way through and I'm falling superfast now. toward the water. but it's not so bad. I'm resting at least. my fairy wings clipped and hanging from the mouths of seagulls above my head.

I hold my arms out. close my eyes. falling like stars falling. and I think to myself *I can be happy like this* as long as I never land. just keep falling with only the air against my skin, I could be happy forever this way.

–I'll always find you– he said to me once. When I told him about my dad. One of the times I was crying. Telling him how my dad didn't look for me. Jay said he would never do that. said it was me and him against the world and nothing could keep us apart.

We've been apart for two days. Two days of asking everyone who might know anything. He wasn't in jail. He never was. Eric tells me that Jay never even got picked up by the cops the night of the raid. He found out from Scott who said he saw Jay today. The cops let him go that night. Told him to get out of their sight and let him walk away while me and Elizabeth sat like animals on the roof three buildings over. While the pee was running down Elizabeth's leg, Jay strolled away just like that. leaving us alone. Leaving me.

He's been staying with people I don't know. In a house over by the river uptown. That's why I haven't seen him. Why Eric hasn't seen him. or anyone for that matter. That's why it has taken two days for me to find out.

I'm going. As soon as I find out, I'm going. Elizabeth comes with me. She's just happy to see me not sulking around anymore. I'm not happy. My stomach's in knots. I can't tell if I'm angry, nervous, or whatever. Probably all. I'm just all messed up because I don't know this part of town. And it's getting scarier. The buildings are getting more and more empty. Not just small squats like downtown. Huge complex buildings. like hospitals. empty. Too big to be empty.

I start to wonder if we're ever going to find Jay. There are so many empty buildings and so few people. Only people we see are homeless. But not homeless kids like us. scary homeless. I hold Elizabeth's hand because the sky is gray and it frightens me. A pigeon flies by our heads and I jump. I'm ready to turn back but then I see them. The old train tracks of the elevated train. The train tracks Eric told me to look for. Look for them arching over the street like a rusted rainbow.

It's at the end of the block. The dead factory where Jay is staying. At least where I was told he is staying. Inside it sounds empty. But it's so big that it's hard to tell. Then I see someone. A kid about my age. I see him and he sees me and doesn't say anything, just nods so that now I know I'm in the right place.

I feel myself starting to get happy. The fear is disappearing and the happiness is taking over the knots in my stomach. I'm thinking about how happy Jay is going to be when he sees me. How he's going to jump and hug me. And how I'm going to kiss him really slow. A really long kiss and he will smile at me and then I will forgive him for not coming to look for me.

As we get closer to the back of the building, there are more kids. Ten or twenty or so. Most of them are punks. Leather jackets, piercing. you know? colored hair and all. It's not our crowd. Not mine and Elizabeth's. we don't fit in. we know we don't fit in. we know because of the looks we get as we walk over the sleeping bodies, trying to find Jay.

–Is Jay here?– I ask some of them. They don't even acknowledge me. Don't even look at me when I ask them. They think I'm stupid. Think I'm someone's little sister looking for her brother or something. Well, fuck them. I don't really care about them. I just want to see Jay. Want to see him right now. and it's as if by wishing so hard I've made my wish come true because I see him. I see him.

He's sitting with a girl on his lap. A girl that doesn't look anything like me. A girl with full breasts falling out of her shirt. With her tongue in his ear like a lizard's tongue.

–*Um, hi.*– he says when he sees me. It's been two days and that's all he can say. A slut in his lap and that's all he says to me. all he says is –*hi*–!

Two nights in that smelly basement. two nights with rats touching up on me and me all freaked out whenever I heard the tiniest sound. two days of worrying myself sick about him. of driving Eric and Elizabeth crazy with my going on and on about how we could just sit here when anything could be happening.

It feels as though my bones will dissolve. as though each time that strange girl's tongue dives into his ear, it shoots into my spine.

I refuse to say anything. just squint at him. my eyes letting him know how angry I am. how hurt. he knows. I know he does because he gets that guilty look on his face. I'm waiting. my arms on my hips, tapping my foot, waiting. waiting for an explanation. an excuse. for anything more than –*um, hi.*– he owes me that much.

Elizabeth digs her fingernails into my arm. pushing me to say something because it's too quiet in here. I look at her. let her know to stay out of this for right now because I'm pissed off.

–Yeah. I didn't know where you were, you know?– he says.

–I didn't know you were ALIVE!– I scream.

I can't believe he didn't come find me. I guess I thought I meant more to him than I do. thought he was different, that he meant it when he promised me he'd find me.

–It's not like we're married– he says and the girl in his lap laughs. Laughs louder than she ought to just to make her point that he doesn't belong to me anymore. that he belongs to her.

–Hey, you're not mad are ya?– and he even laughs when he says it. The faceless others are all laughing. I try to look at them. My eyes are spinning around to catch onto one that I might know. one that will comfort me. Spinning and spinning. that one face that will make them stop. a lonely face on the couch, or in that bunch over on the other end of the loft. But there's no one. no one here knows who I am.

–I hate you– I say because it hurts so much. I say it and the words burn coming out of my mouth. The kids in the room just laugh. Elizabeth digs her dirty fingernails into my arm. harder than before.

–Why'd you come here if you're just gonna be like that? if you're just gonna stand there hating me.– He's enjoying this. the way all the others think he's so cool. his new friends.

I don't know why he's doing this. what I did. I don't know until the ugly girl in his lap speaks. *–Yeah, what do you want here, prude?–* and then I know. I know then that he's told this stranger everything about us. I know by the way she smiles her purple lipstick smile. I know by the way she licks his cheek that she's had sex with him. I know it by the way his arm rests so comfortably around her waist. No longer unsure of himself. No longer clumsy about it like he was with me. No longer sweet. Only ugly.

–Chan, look, I don't think this is gonna work . . . you should go probably.–

I can't say anything because I can't really breathe. it's too hard to breathe trying to hold back the tears. I WON'T let him see me cry. But he's not looking at me anymore. He's turned away. turned back to the girl who swallows his face. Turned back to the people I don't know. the people he's decided are cooler than me. and I feel like an idiot. standing here.

How long do I stay? how long before I run out like a scaredy cat? there's no point in staying any longer, but I can't help feeling that if I stand here, somehow he'll understand. somehow he'll suddenly snap out of it and the Jay I know will come back. come running up to me with a big hug and an I'm sorry.

Eric was right to tell me not to come here. that if Jay hadn't found me there must be a reason and I'd only get hurt. I wish I could forget people the way he does. the way he forgot Lily. And not just Lily. but how he forgot everyone when he came here from California. how he forgot about Marc and Ty after a few weeks of being here. how he almost forgot about me the day Elizabeth and I moved out. I wish I could forget about Jay that way. I wish I didn't have to watch him ignoring me like I don't exist anymore.

Elizabeth wants to leave. more than anything, she wants to. pulling on my hand like a little kid that's gotta go. I want to leave too, but I also don't want to leave at the same time. I don't want to end it this way.

My eyes are all hot. wish I could shoot fire from them and watch everyone burn up. the girl with her lizard tongue lipstick. the faceless kids on the couch. Every last one of them. Even Jay. Wishing they would just go up in flames. nothing but ashes all over the place and I could open the window wide and watch them blow away. I see them snickering. making fun of me. And I can't believe he won't stand up for me. that he can possibly like them more than me in such a short time. I keep thinking that maybe if I stay, maybe just a little longer, it will all be different. it will all be okay.

Elizabeth is whining now. tugging at me. I'm almost ready. but then I hear one of them. One of the ugly strangers. not trying to keep it a secret that we should leave anymore, I hear one of them say *–who the hell brought the brat, anyway? it's like baby school in here.–* my ears are burning. pounding. but I can still hear them. hear him. hear Jay laughing along. and I have to leave fast. have to leave before I let them know that they can get to me.

–Get outta here, girl! You ain't wanted no more!– her purple lipstick voice chasing me the whole way back through the empty factory. Through the empty streets with empty warehouses as my feet barely touch the ground.

Why does everyone in my life turn out to be so rotten? My dad. Jef. and this with Jay. all of the boys really. all of them I've ever known end up being jerks. that's why we're not going back to Eric's. I'm not giving him the chance. because I know he would let me down if I did. because I can't take another person letting me down right now. not for a long time.

I'm going to make a clean break.

I won't speak to any of them ever again. determined not to. We'll leave here soon. me and Elizabeth. We'll leave for our dream in the country. Our own trees and our own sky. We won't need them then. won't need friends. especially ones like them who turn on you when they're finished with you. We'll be just fine by ourselves. alone. we'll be okay that way. better that way. At least, that's what I'm hoping. walking down the street with my eyes so blurry I can't see, that's what I'm thinking.

We can hide here. We can pretend we are almost happy here. In a different place. Here in Chinatown. The streets stretch out in front of us, and as far as you can see there are signs I will never be able to read. Strange faces speaking in strange languages. it feels safe to be so anonymous.

I walk past the stores that sell a hundred different things that all smell like rotten fish. creepy little stores. they make me gag and I turn my nose up and the men that work there laugh when they see me do that.

I have to walk 15 minutes to get anywhere that feels like a real place. I have to walk at least that far before the signs change. before I get where anyone might recognize my face. It's like we went somewhere else. some other city in some other country. in the center of Chinatown. Away from the ghosts. from the shells of my friends, which are empty now. nothing under their skin anymore. Nothing except bones.

I can be anyone I want as long as I'm here. I can be brave if I want to. I can be independent and strong and pretend it doesn't hurt when I think about them. About Jay. Eric. my friends. Ha! some friends! I'm better off. We are better off. me and Elizabeth. We're better off alone in Chinatown. Ancient dragons and things to protect us, like the spooky fish hanging in the glass when I pass by the shop windows. Better off with them than with tattoo dragons.

We're better off now where we're staying. We have running water and a real bed. hot water that comes out when you turn the handle. Sure, it's not free or anything, but it's worth it. We rented a room from this old guy and his family. paid him $100 for the month. It's a lot of money. I don't mind, though. it feels like a home.

They don't bother us none. the guy and his wife and their two little girls. Only the guy speaks any English anyway. The others, I think, are a little afraid of us. I heard them arguing the other night. the man and the woman. she doesn't trust us. doesn't trust us because we're American and not Chinese. I don't think they're here legally, but I would never say anything. like I care. I'm not exactly here in accordance with the stupid law. And that's another thing. I don't think she likes that we're underage. thinks we'll bring trouble. but I think they need the money more.

It's getting dark. I look up as I'm walking. watching the lights turn on all over town. one goes on and then one across the street goes on too. like they're dancing with each other. It's sad, though. how easy it is for those lights to get along. dance arm in arm and leave me below to watch.

Sometimes I find myself reaching for someone's hand. Someone who isn't there. like now. I'm reaching down but no one's hand is there reaching back for mine. I'm alone. Not even Elizabeth's hand is there. She's back in our room. Usually it's hers I'm reaching for. wanting to hold on. I mean, hold on to her literally so she doesn't fall away like the other people. like the other hands that are NEVER there reaching for mine. like Jef's. like Jay's. sometimes like my dad's. only sometimes.

I walk along anyway. alone, I guess. more lights on in the windows. more cars heading over the bridges. I won't be alone for long. It gets crowded around here at night. In Chinatown. People come from all over the place and crowd the streets. the restaurants. the tiny shops that sell tea and weird souvenirs. They spend money and then they leave and the streets seem empty without them. no one left. no one left to leave a handful of coins in my palms while I smile falsely at them.

But before then, before they all get in their nice cars and taxicabs, we have made more money than we ever made downtown. No competition here. none of the other kids like us. they don't figure there's anything to be gained begging here. figure immigrants are worse off than us homeless are, so none of them come. but they forgot about the restaurants and the tourists. that it's easier to get to someone on a full stomach than it is to get to people on their way home from work.

It's getting late. getting way past dark. yeah, it's great in the evening, but everyplace gets a little stranger after it gets really late. I don't feel quite safe. I feel more like a target than anything else. that's why I'm heading home. why it's so nice to actually have a home even if it's only temporary. why I don't mind spending 100 valuable dollars for it. for Elizabeth to have a place to sleep.

I don't go to the parks much anymore. not since we moved here about a month ago. not since I decided I never wanted to see anyone ever again. Not since then have we gone much of anywhere. Maybe that's why we said yes. Why we said we'd go out with him when we ran into Ty. It was kind of nice to see him and I guess I just got caught up in it for a minute.

He looked good. Not like the last time I saw him. a few months ago when he was wasted and sleeping on the sidewalks every night. He didn't look real then. More like a negative that no one ever developed. He didn't look so pale today. Looked almost like his old self. Almost.

I asked him about Jef. I didn't really want to. I didn't want to care, but I did. Besides, last I knew Ty was the only one who still knew if he was alive or not. I had to ask.

–*Yeah, I seen him earlier today. Yeah, he's good.*– It felt nice to hear that. I guess I've been kind of worried, I just didn't realize it.

Ty kept looking around. over his shoulder and every-thing. He rubbed his hands together like it was cold. It's not. still feels like summer. late summer anyway. But he kept rubbing his hands together as he spoke. –*I'm seeing him tonight as a matter of fact*– he said and that's when he invited us to come to the show tonight. said it would be fun. promised. said Jef would be glad to see me.

Elizabeth answered before I could. she promised him we'd be there. –*I'm going to hold you to it little lady*– he said and that made her smile. What could I do? we had to go. Actually, I was kind of excited to go. I guess I was getting over my whole hating everybody thing. It was about time for it anyway. and besides, I hadn't seen Elizabeth so excited in weeks. I guess I never thought about it, but they were her friends too. it wasn't really fair. I guess she missed them more than I thought she could.

Now that we're getting ready, though, I'm real nervous. I mean, what if none of them want to see me? I change my clothes. then change back again. nothing fits right. nothing looks right. nothing feels special enough. impressive enough. then I think I'm just crazy, trying to impress a group of people that go to the bathroom in the streets. I mean, really. I'm just being stupid. I mean, these are my friends, aren't they? so I put on my old t-shirt with the daisy on it and that's that. They'll just have to take me as I am.

Elizabeth's been waiting for me for like an hour. tapping her feet and everything. she's pretty impatient. she really wants to go. has makeup on and everything. but it doesn't matter how much makeup she wears, she still looks young. younger even because it doesn't look right on her. looks cute, though. like playing. I'm ready. but I'm still not sure about the whole thing.

–Elizabeth, I don't know. Maybe we shouldn't go, huh?– I say because I feel sick to my stomach a little. like that first day of school feeling, you know?

I keep picturing myself there, being stupid. not knowing what to say or how to act. I have nothing to talk about. nothing interesting. It would be so much easier not to go. *–Please, I don't want to go.–*

–Why?– Elizabeth snaps. Her voice gets all snotty so that I'm surprised. *–I knew you wouldn't let us go!–* she says, rolling her eyes at me all mean and stuff.

I don't know why she cares so much. It's just a stupid show. But she's so angry at me. I can feel it. It's a worse feeling than the one I had before when I thought we were going. it's worse than the nervous feeling because this one is mean. like it's melting me.

–We never do ANYTHING!– she complains. –Just sit here. Every day! Sit, sit, sit in this dumb room.–

–So?– I don't have any expression. just blank I guess. I know she's right. since Jay. I mean, since he did what he did, I haven't felt like ever having a good time. being social, you know. But I don't like the way Elizabeth is talking to me. I don't. so I guess I get a little mean too. –So, what?– I snap back at her.

–So . . . it's dumb! It's just a small stupid room. It's not like a house or anything special so I don't know why you like it here so much!–

She stood there staring at me. arms folded. eyes bent all angry.

I've never seen her act like this. I don't want this. I don't want her hating me like I hate my mom. my stepmom, I mean. I feel horrible. I feel like she thinks I'm worthless. that everything I've done for her is worthless.

I have to stop myself. because I'm feeling like a mom. I don't want to be her mom. I don't want to treat her that way. I sure don't want her treating me that way!

I have to make it right. I have to make the move. to compromise. I have to let her make some of the choices for both of us. I have to or she'll end up hating me and I couldn't stand myself if she hated me. so I let her decide. –*What do you want to do?*– I ask.

–*I want to go!*– she says. still angry. it's okay, though. It was a stupid question. But I had to ask. –*I want to have some fun*– she says a little softer. Her clean eyes suddenly sad. and I've been so selfish. keeping her cooped up here because it's what I wanted. because it was my dream but not hers.

–*Okay.*–

–*Okay? Really?*– she asks and I nod my head.

Elizabeth claps her hands. just once. She throws her jacket on. throws her shoes on and she's ready to go. She's trying to fake being mad at me still, but she's not. she's trying not to, but she's smiling. I get up slowly. –*Come on!*– she says because I'm taking too long.

We walk through the front rooms. we don't say anything. The mother looks at us. the Chinese woman. she's so unfriendly. I won't even look at her. but I hear her say something to the father. the man we rented the room from. He says something back. it's about us. I don't have to speak Chinese to know that. Oh, well. I don't really care. I mean, we didn't ask them to take our money. to take us in. We're paying for the room, not for parents.

When we finally get outside, it's nice. it's cool. It will be fall soon. I can smell it not too far off. we'll need to get winter coats. if we're going to be staying, we'll need them. But I'm not going to think about that tonight. I promised myself. I'm going to concentrate on having a good time. Because it's tonight that matters. Yesterday mattered but not anymore. Tomorrow doesn't. I have to stop waiting for it. I have to live for today. Elizabeth does. That's all that matters.

I can't hear anything. there's so many people that I can't see anything either. everyone's taller than me. everyone screaming over the music. I don't see anyone I know. I don't see Ty. I don't see Jef. I keep Elizabeth right next to me because I'm afraid I'll lose her too. that I would never find her again in here.

The music's pretty awful. some band that doesn't know how to play any instrument and the singer just yelling into the microphone. I don't know how much of it I can take. not if Jef's not here. not if the whole reason we came vanishes. It's not worth staying then. But I can wait. a little longer. I can wait because Elizabeth doesn't seem to mind.

We've circled around the place a few times. It's not that big to begin with. I still don't see them. I'm a little worried like maybe we missed them or something. Then I see Jef. just for a second before he disappears again behind all the people all over the place. I don't shout. He'd never hear me. Besides, I see him going back through the door that I saw him come out of.

I'm trying to go over there. I tap Elizabeth and she follows me. Pushing through the people, I feel like I'm swimming. like I'm drowning. like I'm being swallowed up by them all moving and turning their shoulders and blocking me from going anywhere. Somehow we make it to the other side of the club where the door is. where it's locked. marked KEEP OUT!

I'm pounding on the door and kicking at it because no one's opening it. No one can hear me, I'm pretty sure. So I hit it harder. faster. –*Fucking knock it off!*– I hear someone yell on the other side. hear the bolt slip from its place and see the handle turn. see Jef's eyes staring at me. taking their time in recognizing me.

–*Holy shit!*– he says then. after he knows it's me for sure. I'm sure I'm smiling wider than I ever have in my whole life. He looks so happy to see me and the nervous feeling I had in my stomach was all for nothing because he grabs me in his arms. lifting me off my feet. hugging me so hard I can hardly breathe. And I feel like an angel for a second. For a second, I forget about the last time I saw him and it's like I've never been apart from him even for a minute.

He puts me down. turns to Elizabeth who's glowing like the stars glow. –*Come here you*– and he lifts her up in the air too. spins her around like a little kid. her skirt like a ballerina's. legs in the air. Jef twirling her around like he's her big brother.

He steps away from the door and it swings open like slow motion. I see their faces appear one by one. people I don't know, but who don't seem surprised to see me. sitting in chairs placed around in a circle. I see Ty. He's sitting in a chair too. The room is dim. smoky. Jef steps into the room and we follow him and he locks the door again behind us.

I kind of stay by the door. I don't know why. I just feel weird going into their circle without really knowing any of them. They look so busy. so secretive or something. something in the way they are looking at me maybe. like they don't want me to disturb them. So I don't. I stay close to the door instead.

It's the first thing I notice. the quiet. It's so much quieter in here I think I've just walked through a door to another planet or something. *–It's so quiet–* I say to Jef but he doesn't answer. Maybe he didn't hear me. I don't see how, though, I mean, with all the quiet. Elizabeth is standing too, next to me.

My eyes kind of burn because I'm not used to the smoke. like a thousand cigarettes of smoke. Elizabeth coughs once. a small cough. She has her hand over her face, covers her mouth. her nose. rubbing her eyes with her fingers. wiping her snotty nose. It makes me giggle to myself. not out loud. It's only funny to me.

I'm wondering if they're going to just leave us standing here. But as I'm wondering, Ty gets up. comes over to us. I breathe easier then. It was getting uncomfortable. I mean, after saying hi, Jef just went back to sitting down. like we never even showed up. But now Ty is trying to make up. He wants us to meet everyone.

His eyes are all red. bloodshot. All of them are that way. it's kind of freaky, but whatever. I don't let it bother me. I mean, I'm here to have fun, right? not judge them for being high or whatever they are. doesn't matter to me.

–*Everyone. This is Chan. And this, this is Elizabeth.*– a few of the guys, they are all guys, a few of them nod. It's funny, I expect slightly more of an introduction. Ty knows that. That's why he whispers to me that none of them really matter. that he doesn't really know all of them him-self. –*Come on*– he says. –*I'll introduce you to some of my friends.*–

We go down a hallway in the back. It's dark. narrow and all. Ty knocks on the door at the other end. Then he opens it. I didn't notice, but Jef has followed us. is standing next to me. covering his mouth. keeps moving his hands around kind of nervous-like. I think maybe it's just because he's high or something. because it's so smoky maybe. Still, it makes me kind of nervous.

There are two men in there. maybe 25 years old. skeevy though. One of them is with a woman. She's pretty. very pretty. like a model. almost perfect. This room, it's the one guy's office. the guy who owns the place. I feel real uncomfortable. the way the three of them are just sitting there staring at all of us. staring at me and Elizabeth. but Ty goes over to them and everyone kind of relaxes. I feel better then.

–Hey, hey, mister Todd! I want you to meet an old friend.– then he comes back and puts his arm around me. walks me over to the desk where the man is. the Mister Todd. Todd is his first name. it's just a thing Ty does. calls people Mister. and their first name.

–This is, uhh, this is our friend. Chan.–

–Nice to meet you– I say. I hold out my hand. He takes it. softly. Then lets it go. And I realize how much I hate adults. how much they don't understand how completely weird they are.

–How nice– he says. He's dirty but his eyelids are clean. clear. white eyelids. His suit is clean. ugly, but new. His skin's pulled all tight against his forehead. Bet he has a clean skull. bleached, maybe.

He lights another cigarette even though the one he has is still lit in the ashtray. The other guy. The woman. They don't say anything. Neither does Ty.

I feel strange again. I see Jef all fidgeting. See Elizabeth covering her mouth. her nose. rubbing her eyes again. –So, Chan?– he says to me. –You are good friends with Ty and Jef?–

–Sure– I say. I don't trust him enough to say anything else.

There are other chairs in the room, but he doesn't offer us any. I think that's rude. Ty and Jef don't make to sit in any of them either. and that's how I know they barely know this guy. I can smell it on them. I know by the way this man looks at them. know because the second guy has gotten up. moved over by the door.

–Well, Chan. Perhaps we should discuss just how good friends you all are?– the tone of his voice makes my stomach turn. I watch him tap the ashes onto the floor. I dart my eyes at Jef and he's looking at the floor. so is Ty. THOSE ASSHOLES! I know something's up. I know it's bad. THOSE FUCKING ASSHOLES!

I don't care what it is, I'm not going to freak out. I can't. If I do I know there's no chance I'll get out of whatever it is they've set me up for. but I'm real scared. like when you get called into the principal's office in grade school, only like six billion times worse. I look at Elizabeth and see her eyes scanning the room. biting her nails. thinking. she knows too. knows whatever this is, it isn't that good. it isn't going to be fun like they promised.

I gotta act cool, though. gotta act like I know all about it. about why I'm here. about the very thing I have no idea about and is driving me insane. I tell myself I'm overreacting as usual. maybe it's just a joke. just Jef and Ty getting back at me a little for not talking to them much lately. But I doubt it. don't really believe it myself, but I try to make myself believe it. try to play along.

–*Yeah, let's*– I say. Then I sit down in the chair across from him. like we're talking about a business deal or something. like they do on the television. Because I don't want to stand anymore. Because my legs are shaking and I can't let them see that.

–*Well, well! You do not disappoint, Miss Chan.*– he's laughing. that kind of real deep laugh that you never really see people have but he does. He scares me. like he just stepped out of somewhere fake, but he doesn't even know it.

I will NOT look at them. at Jef or Ty. They're not look-ing at me anyway. too ashamed, I hope. I hope they're dying inside right now. that they're wishing they had just killed themselves over this, whatever trouble it is they're in, rather than bring me and Elizabeth into it. But they're not. I know they're not. Maybe for right now they might. I mean, this very second. while it's all happening. But they won't once they leave. once they can't see us anymore. They will forget about us and just think about how they're off easy. I know this. That's why I won't look at them. Not ever again.

It's all about money of course. They owe this Todd creep money. lots and lots of money. that's how he puts it. –*Lots and lots.*– I guess they expect me to pay it for them. How could they? I'm so angry. That's our money! Our ticket to get out of here. so we can live like real people. What gives them the right? It's ours!

But then I remember. I remember that they don't know we have any money. How did they find out? I didn't tell anybody. I look over at Elizabeth, but she isn't following. doesn't catch on. It had to be her. but I don't believe it. she would never do that.

–*We've arranged for them to let you pay.*– I KNEW IT! I knew that's what they wanted. why Ty was being all nice and stuff. why he said he was worried when we showed up a little bit late. I knew he didn't care about me that much. knew he didn't really care at all if I came tonight if he wanted me to come just to hang out.

Todd keeps talking. My eyes are burning still. not from the smoke, though. They are burning because I'm soooo mad. —*You see, it doesn't matter to me who does the paying. Just that I get paid, you understand.*— I keep quiet, but I'm burning up inside. wondering how much it is going to cost me. wondering if there is any way out of this. maybe only like a hundred bucks or something. I guess I can handle that much. But I have to know before I agree to help them.

—*How much?*— I ask.

He thinks about it for a second. scratches his tight skull. He is so dirty, so greasy. It's disgusting. —*I don't know. The both of you? Maybe three years. Maybe more. I haven't quite decided on that yet.*—

My mouth falls open. I'm looking everywhere. up. down. I feel like an animal. like I'm in a cage and if I don't break out I'll just curl up and die. The man laughs while he looks at me. —*So. You're not stupid after all.*— I get what he wants from us. Then he looks at her. at Elizabeth standing there in her skirt. her hands rubbing her mouth. his eyes looking at her in a way that makes me sick. I want to tear his eyes out of his head. *–What about you?–* he says to her. *–You don't get any of this, do you, princess?–*

–DON'T TALK TO HER! DON'T EVER FUCKING TALK TO HER!– I scream. not even controlling the words. they're just coming. I can't control my voice. screaming. looking at his eyes. ugly eyes. white eyelids. bleached. I'm bleeding. my brain. bleeding and it's all hot so I can feel it.

–Shhhh, shhhh– Ty is trying to calm me. trying to fucking calm me! he has no right. he. he. fuck him! He has no right to ever speak to me again.

I slap his arm away. hysterical. I slap him again and again until I'm just doing it and I can't stop. yelling at him to GET AWAY FROM ME, to leave, to get out of my face because I'm going to throw up for real. I can't stop until the second guy grabs my arms. holds them to my sides.

I've never been so afraid in my whole life. not the night I spent in the hospital. alone. when I was 5 because I needed tests or whatever. not the first night I came here. not ever. not when my mom died even and I was up the whole night crying and screaming. I'm shaking. my arms

190

are. my knees. my stomach's all turning over and I think I'm going to start crying. trying really hard not to, but it's coming anyway. it's the only thing I want to do. to cry. only I wish I had someone to come and hug me after. someone like my daddy because I've never missed him like I miss him now.

The one night, years and years ago. after my mother had died, after I was over it or thought I was. sitting on my porch, the stars were so bright that night I remember. cold. even though it was summer, it was cold. at least I remember it being cold. it was cold when my dad came out and put his arms around me. he didn't say anything to me, but it's funny how I think we never said more than we did then. that's what I want right now. to curl up on our porch and watch the stars. watch them dive and jump all across the sky while I'm safe and stay there watching them.

But it's him who has his arm around me. Todd. touching me. I shiver every time he puts his hand on my shoulder. scared. shivering under his sweaty hands. I don't move. I can't. I won't do anything for him. he'll have to kill me first.

I keep my eyes closed. Everything's spinning. so fast. Ty and Jef's faces. spinning as they sit in the corner, their heads looking down. I keep them closed. my eyes. keep them shut up real tight so I don't have to see his dirty hand move across my chest.

I don't see her. Elizabeth. I don't see her biting her thumb. I don't see her, but I hear her shoes clapping this way. hear her run a few steps before she kicks him. his shins. kicking until he falls onto his knees. Kicking him so many times after that. so many times and no one in the room has time to realize what's going on. I'm afraid. Afraid the other man is going to come over and kill us. So I get up while Elizabeth picks up something. I never even see what it is. not when she holds it in her hands. not when she hits him across the face with it. not when it falls from her hands when he falls to the ground.

No matter how many dreams I have where I'm wearing fairy wings. no matter how often I'm floating through the sky. however unreal it seems. it's still not as strange, as dreamlike, as I feel running through the hallway. not hearing any sound. like moving through water. the door still open behind us. I look back and I can see his head on the floor. the blood around it. his clean, bleached skull and I run like I'm flying.

like in my dreams where I'm falling so slowly from the roof of tall buildings and drifting down like an angel.

I'm sure I'm going to trip and fall. it's so dark. I don't feel my legs. don't hear a sound. blood on Elizabeth's chin but she wipes it off as we run. into the other room and past the boys sitting in their chairs. caught in their private dreams and barely noticing us. barely awake. their eyes like clouds. zombies.

Slowly. Sound is getting into me again. slow. Sounds of the music on the other side of the door as I'm working on the lock to get it undone but my hands are shaking. sound of chairs moving against the floor, metal scratching metal. made-up sounds like the sound of him getting up and running down the hall but he's dead. Elizabeth's pushing me. shoving me out of the way. I'm sorry. no matter how hard I try, nothing I do will cause the thin bolt to slide from its place. I'm sorry, Elizabeth. sorry I'm not doing anything to help you. that I made you do everything.

She moves so quick. I blink and I miss it. miss her opening the door and it's open. the music suddenly so loud I can hear nothing anymore. seeing her disappear into the flood of people. all moving. like animals. like insects. moving together. against each other. I wipe my eyes and I see her.

there. right there. getting myself together. getting my feet to move and I'm right behind her. sweating. pushing the hair out of my face. pushing the people out of the way because if I don't make it to the door I will drown. I will die.

I don't see him until I feel my hair being pulled. my head snapping back. the other guy from the room. spinning me around. facing me. shoving his hand in my face because I'm screaming. and I don't know what's happening when the guy next to him, a stranger, punches him in the face. –*Fuck are you doing to her, man*– standing over him so that he doesn't get up and I run. tripping and struggling. getting through. getting to the front door and outside. fresh air hitting me like cold water. like something new. like a promise of something else.

We don't go home. don't go anywhere, just keep running because we've run our whole lives. running until we can forget what happened. until it fades with the sidewalk we leave behind. until we pass enough buildings, enough stores, enough parked cars.

I can't run anymore. I can't breathe. I stop. stand there. Elizabeth runs halfway down the block before she notices.

before she stops. I'm bent over. panting. my hands on my knees, looking up at her. she's breathing heavy too. all flushed. she looks so pretty. so strong. her voice is so young. –Chan?– she says. –Chan?– then she's in my arms. crying. her chest, in and out, in and out, over and over. her whole body shaking. her whole body is crying.

I sink to the sidewalk. lowering her in my hands. her head resting in my lap and we sit there like the stars just sit in the sky above the switched-on city.

I move the hair from her eyes. holding it back on her shoulders so she can cry as much as she wants. lying in the middle of the sidewalk. The people all walk by us. they don't stop. they look, but they don't stop. they're all faceless. all made-up people. I glare at them with angry eyes. staring while Elizabeth keeps her eyes closed. her head in my lap. her legs naked against the cement. all scratched up. all pretty.

My eyes are puffy. hers too. messy. but we're safe now. for right now. we can sit here like strangers for as long as we want. And I feel weightless. like I will float away. drift higher and higher over us. looking down. like a beautiful painting.

Elizabeth is shivering. breathing normal again. I wrap her up tighter in my arms. like my dad did that one night.

it's the same thing. same like how we don't say anything but are speaking tons to each other. spots of blood on her shirt. tiny spots, but I see them and they make me sad. I want them to disappear. want to make them disappear by touching them. So I run my finger over them. But they don't disappear. they're still there when I take my hand away. I can still see them. still see them in the reflection of her eyes.

And we sit there. perfectly still. breathing in and out at the same time like we've melted together. like Siamese twins, and I wish we were sometimes. wish we shared the same body sometimes. then she'd always be with me. would never leave. I wouldn't worry about her so much like I'm worrying now. worried she won't need me much longer. not after tonight. not after I didn't do anything to stop it. not after she was so tough. Now I know that I need her more. maybe more than she needs me. I love her. I thought it was always me, that she needed me, but I guess I was wrong. It is me. me that needs someone. that needs her. for the rest of my life, I think I'll need her.

Elizabeth wants to leave right now. to grab our things and take off into the night. We're in our room. It's not home, I know that now. it's just a room. I want to go too, but I don't know where we'll go. I don't want it to be because of them. because of what happened. That would spoil the whole thing. I don't want it to be like this. to be scared off. It was supposed to be a happy thing. like waking up with the sun shining on our faces and we decide it's the perfect day. not in the middle of night. not because we're looking over our shoulder everywhere we go because we're so scared there's someone there. chasing us.

We came back here. Everyone was asleep. was. I think they've probably woken up by now. with Elizabeth scream-ing. yelling at me because I say we should wait. that she's just a little kid and doesn't know we need to wait. at least until tomorrow. until morning comes. She gets mad at me. I know she does. But I'm right. I know I am.

–NO!– she is still screaming. I want her to stop. to be quiet. to stop being a baby. I don't want our Chinese land-

197

lord and his wife to wake up and start yelling at us in strange words. to start asking questions and calling the police and everything. *–I want to leave. RIGHT NOW!–*

And I see her clearly now. the frilly skirt bunched up around her waist like playing dress-up. the bottom of her kitten printed underwear. how small her eyes are. her nose. everything about her. I see her move to put her hand to her mouth before she stops. see how she has to concentrate on not putting her thumb in her mouth when she sleeps. see how 11 years old she really is.

It's like my heart is breaking. seeing her this way. It's like that because I cannot pretend anymore. can't pretend that we're a happy family. can't pretend everything's okay or that I can protect her from all these awful things.

Maybe. maybe if I can just get her to go to bed. maybe tomorrow this horrible feeling will go away. Tomorrow. Everything will be better tomorrow. She'll see I'm right then. If we just let it pass.

–We'll leave tomorrow. Okay?–

–NO. Not okay. You promised!–

–*There's no trains this late anyhow. There's nowhere to go!*– I say. I'm trying to stay calm. to not lose my temper. I feel like I'm talking to a small child. Her pale fists curled up like angry paws. I feel like I'm talking to a little kid and if I lose my temper I will lose the argument.

–*I don't care*– she says out of the corner of her mouth. biting the words at me.

I sit down on the bed. sit down beside her. I'm quiet like my mom used to be when I was upset. sitting there until I calmed down. I wait. wait. wait.

–*Let's go to sleep?*– I whisper nicely. softly. But too soon. I didn't wait long enough because she's still mad at me.

–*No!*– she says. –*Un-uh, I'm not going to sleep. I want to go. You promised we could go!*–

–*I know, but*– I'm keeping my voice down. nice and soft because she's being really loud and I don't want everyone to wake up. because I want my tone to rub off on her. I want her to calm down. to listen to me. –*I mean, I want to go too. But we need to wait. I promise, we'll leave in the morning. Okay, squirt?*–

–DON'T CALL ME THAT!– that hurts. it hurts when she says that. I didn't mean anything by it. just wanted things to be like they were. like they were only earlier today. Why is that so bad?

I back away because I can't handle this. not tonight. I shouldn't have to handle this.

But I think she's sorry about it. I think so because she lowers her head. lowers her voice. –*I'm sorry*– she says. –*Just don't call me squirt, okay? Please?*– and my heart breaks into a billion trillion pieces right then. she's grown older. It doesn't matter how little she is. how little she acts. She's older because she's pulling away from me. and that makes me mad. I don't know why. but I'm mad. I'm so mad at her right now. well, not at *her*, but at her not needing me anymore. I know I can't handle taking care of her. that I've failed. I know I can't handle her pulling away from me. because I need her to need me because without that, I'm just nothing. just another white-trash streetkid with nothing.

I'm standing there in my pajamas. staring at her. I feel like the little kid. and that makes me mad too. I bite my lip because I'm afraid I'm going to say something. something really mean that I don't really want to say.

She comes over to me. tries to take my hand. –*Chan, I'm sorry.*– she's whining. I won't let her take my hand. I want to let her, but I don't. just being stupid I guess. I don't even know why I'm mad at her. I should be proud. how brave she was. But I can't be. All I can be is mad. because I don't want her to be brave. I want her to always be my little sister. forever.

She's getting undressed now. putting on her pajamas too. I don't care. I guess I won, but I didn't want to. didn't want to have something to win. I know she's only giving up because I'm being a baby. She's climbing into bed. not really into bed, I guess, just kinda lying on top of the sheets. closing her eyes so she won't have to look at me.

I wait awhile. Then I turn off the light. walk across the room to turn it off and then walk back again. But I don't climb in bed. not right away. I stand on the other side of her. watching her. watching her turn away from me in her sleep. not really sleep, but in her going to sleep. the shadow of her body in the yellow light on the sheets. Through the window next to her, the open window, I see the buildings way across the street. They look fake, like the moon looks fake. like scenery.

I'm not mad anymore. just tired.

tired of always running.

of always being so unsure of everything.

I want to put my arms around her. want to so bad. to hold her like that first night we met. But I just lie there. looking at the back of her head. letting it hurt so much that I'm not letting my hand reach out to touch her hair.

–*I'm not a kid.*– I hear her say. I barely hear it. She mumbles it so quiet, but not quiet enough that I don't hear it at all. and that's worse.

I close my eyes. lying on my back with my hands folded on my stomach. staring up into the space that's there when you close your eyes. getting farther and farther. I feel myself, my body, falling so far away from me. and I'm just rising. into darkness. not a star around me. no wings anymore. no nothing, just me. lonely. cold. so cold. no pretty things. no happy things. no promise of anything left to come.

The sun isn't up yet, but I can't sleep. I have to get up. I am all sweaty, and I don't want to be in bed anymore. late summer kind of hot that doesn't go away unless you get up. get out of this bed where Elizabeth is snoring quietly. like a kitten almost. so softly I think it might drive me crazy.

I'm careful to not make any noise when I get up. The bed creaks, but only once. I'm perfectly still until it stops. until I'm sure it hasn't woken her up. Then I get up. my feet so soft on the wooden floor. moving across the room, across the floor. turning the knob so it doesn't make a sound. doesn't disturb the city that seems to be dead right now in the early morning.

It's not so hot in the other rooms. it wouldn't be so hot in ours if we left our door open at night. have to keep it closed, though. have to, because we are living with strangers who don't know us well enough to see us sleeping. who don't trust us. don't really want us there but will accept us because we've paid up front.

Usually I wouldn't shower this early. I know it will wake up the children. their room is right next to the bathroom. I see them in the bed. their door is open. I see them sleeping. the little one with her mouth open. her eyes closed. I don't look for long.

I make sure the door is closed tight before I turn the water on. make sure the door is locked. Then I get naked, leaving my pajamas in a big pile on the floor. I stand in front of the mirror so that I can look at myself. I'm so ugly. at least I think I am. I mean, I know I'm not really ugly. it's just the way I feel. My face is pretty. I guess I know that.

My hair just sort of hangs there, though. not exactly curly, but not exactly straight either. wavy, I guess. and I can't believe myself. standing here worrying about how I look. I mean, there's other things I could be worrying about. but somehow, I'm glad. I should worry about how I look. I shouldn't have to think about other things. I'm only 15 after all. how I look should be the most important thing in the whole world to me.

It's getting hard to see myself with the steam fogging up the mirror. I wipe it off with my hand. I used to think I was pretty enough. when I was littler. Maybe my nose is too small. makes me look too young. My teeth aren't crooked or anything. I don't have thin lips or nothing. I do have pretty eyes. I love my eyes. But I'm not pretty enough. not the prettiest. Maybe I'm just another girl. just like every other girl in the world and that means no one will ever give me a second look.

I have to wipe the mirror off again. I shouldn't. I should just get into the shower and forget about it. But somehow it makes me feel good to stand here, hating the way I look. makes me feel normal. I move my eyes away from my face. biting my nails. I don't have much of a chest. hardly nothing. I put my hands over them. over my breasts. I have one freckle there. I always thought it was ugly, but for some reason, right now, I think it's the most beautiful part of me. Then it disappears as the mirror gets clouded over again. and I disappear. fade away. disappear into the shower where the water is hot and clean. wash away everything I hate about myself for the time being.

My clothes are soaking wet. I forgot to hang them up while I was taking a shower, so I have to walk back through the apartment with the towel around me. dripping onto the floor. dripping a trail of water behind me with each step. little footprints on the wooden floor.

I don't know what makes me do it. why I even want to. but I want to so bad. I let the towel fall off of me while I'm standing outside our bedroom door. No one's awake so it doesn't matter, but it makes me feel weird. I mean, standing there. I don't open the door right away. just stand there. I feel entirely myself. I feel entirely free from everything.

I stand there for ten whole minutes. my hands at my side. arms at my side. facing the door, wondering if anyone could see me. scared that someone would see me. I feel so dangerous. like I almost want to stand here until someone gets up and catches me. but I don't. I open the door and step inside.

Elizabeth is still asleep. She's moved over. taking up the whole bed even though she's all curled up in a little ball. I'm looking at her face. the way her skin is so pale. so smooth and perfect like doll plastic. her lips are pink when she sleeps. her eyelids are pink too. She's the most extraordinary thing I've ever seen. I'll do anything for her. And I'm sorry I ever got mad at her. ever. sorrier that she got mad at me because we should have left in the night like she wanted. But we will leave today. I just have to take care of a few things first. have to say goodbye to the city first. But we will leave. Today, we will.

I sit next to her on the bed. next to her snoring, but so soft that I can barely hear it. I think it's cute the way she snores. you know, not like an old man or nothing. just little tiny snores. baby snores. My hair is dripping water onto the sheets. I wrap the towel around it so that it won't drip on her. won't wake her up when I lean over and put my hand on her shoulder. when I kiss the back of her head and then stand up. put my clothes on.

The dress slips easily over my shoulders and I let it fall around my knees. pressing it flat with a hand over my stomach. letting my hair stay wherever it falls when I unwrap the towel and drop it on the floor. Elizabeth stirs in bed. I freeze. hold my breath. but she's awake anyway so I let the air out.

–*What are you doing?*– she asks. all sleepy. blinking. stretching her arms over her head. her hands in little fists.

–*morning*– I say. trying not to smile because she might still be mad at me and I don't want to look stupid.

–*morning*– she mumbles.

She's sitting up in bed when I ask her to get dressed. –*What for? Are we leaving?*– and her eyes light up, popping slightly from her head.

–*Not right now*– I say. –*I want to go to the park.*– I want to watch the dawn come up one last time. I haven't for so long and I really want to see the sky that way so that I will remember it like that forever.

–*I don't want to go to any parks*– she says. simple as that. like it doesn't matter. –*why don't we just leave?*– it's a fair question. one I'm not sure how to answer in a way to make her understand. –*We can go somewhere where there's always a park and then it won't matter.*–

–*It's not that*– I say. –*It's . . . I don't know, it's something else.*–

Elizabeth frowns. She doesn't even pretend to get up. She puts her head back on the pillow.

–*Elizabeth?*–

She looks at me. one eye open.

–*Please come with me.*–

She lays there like someone who is sick of talking. She shakes her head. –*I'm not going*– she says and closes her pink eyelids, and I wonder how it is she's grown so independent of me.

–*Please?*–

–*No.*–

–*Fine.*– it's something I have to do. part of me needs to be left there in that park. I need to leave it. –*I won't be long, okay?*– I whisper to her as I lean over the bed. I brush the hair away from her face. –*Okay?*–

–*Sure*– she says.

Before I pull the bedroom door closed, I blow a kiss to her. to where she's sleeping with her face turned away.

It smells like fish. We live next to a shop that sells fresh fish, and it always smells. Sometimes I don't notice it, but today I'm noticing everything for some reason. maybe because I'm alone. but I notice all the little details I've always seemed to miss. the faint smell of saltwater in the air because the ocean is right there, not too far away. the way the clouds seem to be standing still while the sun is trying to move up. it's just an orange light on the horizon right now, but it's struggling, pushing up against the sky. trying to show its face. I'll have to hurry to the park if I'm going to make it.

I decide I'll take the train to be safe. I mean, it's not real far from Chinatown to Tompkins Square Park. close enough to walk, but it will take too long. I can't miss it. Not today.

The park was the first place I went when I came here to the city. not on purpose. not because I wanted to. I was so scared. I laugh about it now. not about being scared. I laugh about that day in the park. How I thought little, 4-block, tiny Tompkins Square was Central Park.

I remember that first day. The sun was coming up and I stood there in the park. my eyes like Christmas, only wider, scareder. so many people I couldn't keep up. people coming from everywhere and I just kept spinning. spinning around in circles. It wasn't until I looked up that I stopped. looked at the sun. It was beautiful, burning the edges of my eyes.

I want to see that one last time. see it exactly like it was that day so I know for certain that I've changed. that I'm ready to leave. I wish I could have explained it to Elizabeth. then maybe she would've come with me.

I have to hurry. It's almost time and I'll miss it completely if I don't hurry.

I walk so fast my legs start burning. fixing my eyes at the end of each block and counting the seconds until I reach it. then I start right over again with the next. I do that until I can see the subway entrance. then I use that. the stairs. I use them to fix my eyes so that maybe I'll reach them quicker that way.

When I'm close, I can hear the train pulling in underground. I race down the stairs. one at a time, but skipping some here and there. getting the token out of my pocket so I'll be ready. so I won't miss the train. hoping that maybe it was the train on the other side. the downtown. but now I see it. see that it's my train.

I'm trying to slip the token into the slot so that I can get through the turnstile, but it falls. I have to bend down to pick it up. should've just crawled underneath, but I didn't. I pick it up and place it in the place that swallows them up and then I go through. Too late.

I watch the lights as the train pulls away. watch them going deeper into the tunnel, turning the corner. the windows on the last car staring at me like ghost eyes. blue sparks of electricity shooting from the tracks as the metal wheels scratch against the metal rails. My life will always be twenty seconds off track because that was the train I was supposed to be on and I might have to spend the rest of life trying to catch up.

There's no one else on the platform. anyone else would have made the last train. But I don't know if anyone was there before. it's so early. not yet time for people rushing off to work. I laugh a little, imagining the train I missed screaming through the tunnels with not a single passenger. a death train. kinda glad I missed it then. Besides, the next one is only one station away. I see its lights like two mechanical eyes staring out through the darkness when I lean over to check.

It races by me. howling. Most of the windows show empty cars. show the glare of the lights inside against the plastic. I'm standing so close, I can almost feel the train touching my hair as the wind blows it around. So I step away. wait for it to stop and wait for the doors to open.

When they do, the air-conditioning feels nice. almost too cold, but nice because it was so hot standing there. I walk in and take a seat. No one next to me, but there are some people on the other side of me. sitting across from me. The train jerks into motion. I'm just along for the ride. letting it take me where I want to go.

It's only two stops away, but I see so much in those two stops. see it because I want to remember it all this way. the city. I want all my memories to be like this morning. I don't want to miss a single second.

I see a little kid with her mom. they stand by the subway doors. waiting for the train to pull into the station. and it does. The doors open. the little girl wrinkles her nose in surprise. she's so confused by the opening doors. no more than 4 years old. And I laugh, thinking that it's kind of silly that something like that can make me laugh. Maybe I was in a good mood before that, but it's hard to tell because I feel like I haven't been in one for such a long time. It feels nice, though. I feel like smiling. at nothing really. just smiling.

There's a man sitting across from me. He's reading the newspaper. He's kind of cute in an older sort of way. He's not old really. I mean, not like 80 or something. maybe 30. but old to me. He's not paying attention, just reading his paper and there is a cute girl sitting next to him. a little younger than him, but not real young. you know, like 20 anyway at least. Asian. She has beautiful eyes beneath her glasses. She's reading too and I know they don't notice each other. But I'm watching them both. They make such a cute couple. Funny how two strangers could be so perfect for each other but don't even know that anyone is even right there next to them.

I want to say something to them. tell them they look cute together so that maybe they will really get together. But this is my stop. The doors are already about to close because I wasn't paying attention. I have to hurry before they close on me and then I'll never see the dawn rise for sure. So I don't say anything to them. They'll just have to figure it out for themselves.

Outside the sky is in so many colors, just swirling around as the gray morning waits and wonders for the sun to come up and push all the blue back into place. It's coming soon. It's right there, just under those buildings. just over a few more avenues. There, the sun is waiting. was waiting for me longer than it should have. but it waited and I'm glad it did.

I'm lying on the grass. it's cool and wet. my hair mixing in with the grass and I'm staring up at the sky through the leaves in the tree that's right next to where I am. watching the skyscrapers like needles touching up on the clouds. the pigeons waddling around on the sidewalk not taking any notice of me, or the sunrise. But once the first glint of daylight hits their beady black eyes, they shoot up like rockets. flapping their wings so hard I can almost see the flapping in the way that the leaves change direction, so slightly.

There's no one around me. just the few people that have spent the night here. sleeping. The whole city is dreaming. I look at the windows. into them. I think I can almost see all their sleepy faces resting on soft pillows. their eyelids shut up tight while the world is coming alive around them. Soon they will all wake up to the sound of alarm clocks ringing. buzzes and beeps and radios switching on by the dozens. the sound of televisions and sirens racing down the street. They will all come alive like some Hollywood set and when someone suddenly yells –ACTION– that will be their cue.

They will come out of their apartment buildings one by one, or in pairs. Some will be dressed for the weather. Some will be wearing three-piece suits regardless, and those are the people I won't understand when I see them. There will be kids off from school because it's summer. They will race to the playground that's right there behind me. They'll go through the gate pushing and tackling to be the first one in.

There will be older kids, kids like me who will be taking their time. walking around. looking for the best way they can waste their day doing nothing at all. And I won't understand them. I can't understand them. their lives. their routines. up at 7:30 am, bed by 11:30 pm. Three meals. wash your hair every other day. Things that all seem so far away from me, from my life, but things they do every day without thinking about it. Our lives are so distant even though we share the same bench in the same park.

The delivery trucks will come soon. They will start driving up and down. back and forth from one store to the next dropping off whatever it is the store has run out of the day before. erasing need. erasing the empty quiet of the streets. The taxis will come. shuffling people from home to work. All the cars will come. They will be here soon.

But right now there is no one. I still have a little while before any of that happens and when it does, I'll be prepared. I'm already imagining it to myself, so when they all come, I won't be surprised by any of it. I won't let any of it sink in. won't allow it to make me think any less of myself. Until then, I will just look. amazed at how pretty it can all be. how sometimes it can all look so ugly, but never in the morning. never when the day is just starting. And I guess it just has to become ugly. that it's just a natural process like evaporation or erosion. When I leave for good, I will try to not remember the ugly parts. only the pretty ones. like this one. right now.

I know now. I know where we will go. Elizabeth and me. I know because the sun shines and it tells me.

We will go to Vermont or somewhere else like it. by a lake somewhere. Sitting here in the park, it's all so clear to me now. That's where we'll go. somewhere wide open. a breeze blowing. the trees. long trees and skinny ones. we'll watch them dancing in the sun. watch them every day forever. It would be like this. like today, here in the park. but not the city to get in the way. not the buildings. not the people looking at me. the cars with gasoline rainbows rising off the blacktop. none of that. Just the trees. the lake. me and Elizabeth. together. watching it all like I'm doing now. but better. always better.

If I close my eyes tight I can see it already. if I close them real tight. The flowers. I can smell them and everything. I want to hold them. pick a whole bunch of them. pretty ones. hold them to my chest, like the cover on some old story. That's what I want. I want it for us. I want it so much my eyes hurt. squeezing them shut so tight I see stars. little sparks against my eyelids.

I can't wait to tell her. to whisper in her ear. whisper the sound of the breeze in her ear like music. so that she can hear it too. She'll be so excited. so happy. I can't wait. can't wait to see her smile move across her face. to see her lip curl over her two top teeth.

I can see the house we will live in. little and blue. I can see the curtains in the windows. dancing. the breeze through the open window pushing them this way and that. From the porch I can see clear across the lake, looking all the way into somewhere else that is unfamiliar. Elizabeth's in front of me. the sun sitting perfectly in her dark hair. smiling. The whole picture blends into one color. more like a feeling I guess. blending. wrapping around me. It's warm and beautiful and I hold on to it.

I don't go back right away. I don't mean to fall asleep but it happens. when the sun is so warm and the grass is so nice because it's not so warm as the sun. I just can't help but fall asleep. my dream like water washing against my feet.

It must be sometime around 2:00 in the afternoon. just guessing, but it must be. from how bright it is. It makes me kind of uneasy. I'm a little worried I'll see someone I know when I walk through the park to leave. it's late enough. I don't want to. I don't want to see anyone I know from here. I've already said goodbye to them in my head. seeing them for real would only make things worse.

So I walk, keeping my head down. running through a list of people I might see. Who would be the worst to see? Eric. Eric would definitely be the worst because he's the only one who would still be there for me if I needed him. the only one I'd still turn to, I guess. I couldn't take seeing him right now. him seeing me running away. I wouldn't want to have to tell him about last night. I don't think I could ever tell anyone about that.

Sure, Jef or Ty would naturally be horrible. but I don't even count them. I don't even count them as people anymore. just bones and skin. there's nothing inside them anymore. nothing inside of me for them.

And as I think of others, more come to me to the point where I can't stop and people I haven't thought about in weeks just pop into my mind. There's so many. circling through my mind that I feel like I'm going to suffocate from

219

all the figures in my head. that I'm sure to run into at least one of them before I get out.

Jay. I keep coming back to him. the others all sort of fade as soon as they come to mind. I mean, Scott and Eva. all the rest of them. they don't stick around. But Jay. I think about Jay. can't stop thinking about him now that I've started. about the silly way he smiled when he used to hold my hand. when he used to like me. all those stupid things he used to say but they always seemed so perfect for whatever was going on. I miss him a little. not him really, but the him that liked me.

I know it's dumb, but somehow, I always thought when today came, when I left I mean, that he would come with me. him, me, and Elizabeth. together like some make-believe family. kind of like Peter Pan and Wendy and those other kids they always took with them. that's how I thought about us. It's just stupid, really. but it makes me kind of sad to remember that.

And then there's Lily. it takes me a long time to get to her. I realize I've almost forgotten about her. almost can't even picture her anymore. It's not so much that I think I'm going to see her here. I mean, no one's seen her since that one night. feels like forever ago. I know I won't see her, but remembering people makes me remember her.

This time tomorrow, I will be just like her. gone. vanished. No one will know anything. won't know what happened to me. They'll piece things together. about the night before. try to figure it all out, but none of them will ever see me again to know for sure. I will be just like Lily is to me. some kind of mystery forever. And that makes me happy. not that I'm going to make people worry about me, if they really are going to worry anyway. but happy because I think about Lily. that maybe nothing bad happened to her. maybe she had the whole thing planned out. maybe she had a whole bunch of money saved up too. maybe she is somewhere wonderful right now. somewhere being the center of attention. She looks really nice. I mean, that's how I'm imagining her. how I will always imagine her for the rest of my life.

It all feels like a dream. standing at the cash register. waiting to pay. I decide to get something to drink. pink lemonade. Butterflies swimming around in my stomach because it's becoming so real to me. standing there in the deli. the cars going by outside. The door is open. looking out. like a window into a movie. like it's all not really there. that I'm just watching something that isn't real. or won't be soon.

And for some reason, I'm afraid to leave. afraid to walk out that door into the street again. to start walking. it's so hot in the late summer sun. walking for the last time back downtown. to our home that's not our home anymore the second we leave the next time.

I feel like I did that day three years ago. sitting in my bedroom at home. Only that was worse. I was so afraid then. my stuff all around me and I knew I wasn't going to take any of it. I wouldn't have gotten past the door if I had. I didn't take anything. just a change of clothes and all the money I could find lying around. the money my dad kept in his dresser.

I sat there for hours. there on my bed. sat there waiting for it to get dark. waiting for my stepmom to fall asleep like she always did in the evening. passed out. she would drink all day and then kind of just die once the sun went down. I waited until then. until I heard her door close. heard her yell at me one last time through my closed door.

I never felt so alone. so old. walking through the living room. the television turned on quietly. the blue glow shining on the walls as I opened the door and stepped through it. I didn't close the door. I left it open. the blue light of the television getting fainter as I walked down the dirt driveway. walked past the tall pines that grew so thick I thought I might get lost before I ever even reached the highway. and when I got there, what then. I would just stand along the side of the road, invisible to the trucks and the cars with all their headlights screaming by. I didn't want to get into any of them. just wanted to walk beside them. to have the comfort of knowing they were there. knowing they were giving me some light to walk by.

The guy at the deli hands me my change. I'm not paying attention. too lost. daydreaming. I drop the coins and they fall behind the counter. He bends down to pick them up. I tell him it's alright. but I don't move. I'm still standing there so he doesn't believe me. picks them up anyway. And I'm so afraid to walk out that door. so afraid I'm just going to be starting all over again. not knowing where I'll be tomorrow or the next day.

She's not there when I get back. I think she's in the shower at first, but there's nothing there. in our room. she's not here. maybe she went to the store or something. getting something to eat. but her things are gone. all her clothes. all her little trinkets she's been collecting. little stones, a stuffed animal, matches. none of it.

But her scent is still here in the room. the smell of her hair. of her breath on the pillow. it's all here. all those tiny things that make up her are here. But she's gone. The money is all gone too. All of it. I check. But I don't believe it, so I check again. and again. Check the closet again. Make sure there isn't really anything of hers here that proves she's coming back. Check the bathroom again. I run back to our room. throw the blankets off the bed, just in case. in case she's playing or something. throw my clothes off the hangers in the closet onto the floor.

I'm hysterical. I'm screaming. The Chinese family is looking at me like I've lost my mind because I think I might be. spinning around in circles so I can see the whole room

225

at once, hoping I missed something. anything. getting dizzy, looking.

–*We thought you gone. She gone.*– I hear the man but I'm not listening to him. I know all that. I'm figuring that out on my own.

–*Didshesaywhereshewent? Didshe? Didshesayanything atall? ANSWER ME, PLEASE!*– but they don't understand anything I'm saying. I'm speaking so fast. so crazy. pounding on the bed so that I can hear the springs breaking. yelling at them.

–*Where? Where?*– I'm trying to speak carefully. still yelling but trying to get the words out one at a time. –*Where? Do you fucking understand that? Where? You know what that means? What where means?*–

looking on the floor because maybe she left a note. because maybe she's planned this. waited for me to leave and left right after me. that's why she didn't want to go. why she didn't stop me from going. Now I'm left behind. looking for a clue. for anything. but there's nothing from her.

The wife is talking really fast to the man. He's shrugging his shoulders. mumbling. It's all foreign so I don't know what they're saying. But I know they haven't answered me yet. So I yell at them again –*WHERE DID SHE GO?*– and the woman starts yelling at the husband again. She hates me. But I'm not going anywhere until they answer.

–*Gone.*– his arms raised to his side so to show me he doesn't know where. Didn't ask. Didn't care.

–*when? when did she leave?*– I ask, quieter now because I can't yell anymore. it's too hard to yell through the tears that are starting up in the back of my throat. my shoulders feel so heavy. I let them fall. My whole body feels so heavy and it's hard to hold it up for long. like my spine is breaking inside of me. my legs turning all soft like my knees have just disappeared or something.

–*When?*– I'm begging.

–*Um. No*– he says. –*Not, uhh. Not breakfast, not long since then. Maybe 2, maybe 3 hour.*– and my heart falls to pieces because that's too long. long enough for her to be anywhere.

The woman is screaming again. screaming at me. But I'm leaving anyway. She doesn't have to scream. I'm going. I'm not coming back. not ever. I don't take anything with me. just head straight for the door. I can hardly feel my legs, but I'm running. leaving them behind me. leaving everything behind me because nothing matters if I can't find Elizabeth. nothing will ever matter again if I can't find her.

Their voices fade with each flight of stairs I go down. cursing me but I can't understand the words so they can't hurt me. already hurting too much for anything to hurt me more. not even a gunshot could hurt me right now. too much pain to feel any new pain. that's how I am. how I am when I reach the bottom of the last step and stand outside looking both ways because I have no idea which way to go. where to start.

Maybe if I'd listened to her. not her words, but to the things she didn't say. the secrets she kept inside so that I could never know everything she felt. I should have climbed into bed with her. put my arms around her to watch the sunrise from our window. and I could've quietly stolen those secrets from her. maybe if I had done just one little thing different then everything would be different. maybe if I didn't keep saying no to her. at everything she wanted to do. maybe if I hadn't said no last night, then I know I could've changed this.

I'm losing it so bad right here on the sidewalk. people bumping into me because I'm wandering around. tilting. my hands covering my face. –*Watch it*– and bumping into me, pushing me in some other direction but I don't care. I wish I hadn't been so selfish. that I had held her tight and never let her go because now I don't know if I'll ever be able to touch her again.

I'm going to all the places, the last places where I knew people to have been staying. praying she went to one of them. that she was just mad at me like she gets sometimes. telling myself she would never really leave without me.

But I can't find anybody. All the squats have been closed down in the last few months and I don't know where people are staying anymore. I didn't follow them. People are staring at me because I'm screaming her name and crying, running down the streets. one after the other and just screaming her name over and over. pulling my hair and my hair is a mess but I don't care at all about any of that. can't believe I wasted time this morning caring about that when I should have been spending one last second with her.

I was so afraid of running into someone earlier and now I absolutely can't find a single face that might recognize me. All I see are strangers and all I want to see are people I know. anyone that she might have seen. that might have said something to her or at least seen her. seen which way she was going so I could go that way and try to catch up with her. to grab her and hug her. tell her I love her and that she can never leave me again like this.

The only thing I can hear is the sound of my own voice bouncing off the buildings. echoing her name back to me.

Then I give up on finding her out here. I have to find her where she's leaving. Grand Central. She always wanted us to leave from Grand Central Station. Didn't matter that you could only go north from there. didn't matter where she went, only mattered where she left from. and that makes me cry. hearing her tell me that again in my head. telling me the story about her coming to the city as a little girl. getting off the train and seeing the tall ceiling in Grand Central. how beautiful it was to her. how special. like magic. how her dad slapped her because she took too long staring up at the painting of stars on the ceiling and how that's why she wanted to leave from there. to take as much time as she wanted to look up. to walk through there her own way.

That's the only thing that keeps me going. keeps me breathing without just wanting to stop and let all the air seep out of me forever. Maybe if I can get there in time, she'll be there. in the middle of that giant hallway. staring up with her two ponytails hanging loose at the center of her back. I just have to get there. But I don't have any money. don't have any tokens for the subway. I have to walk and it's so far away. I want to give up but I won't let myself give up. I start walking. running. watching the streets count off as I pass each sign at each corner. running for her. running for the chance to see her one last time so that she can see me. see how sorry I am for anything I did that might have made her hate me. so that she will change her mind because I need her. will always need her forever.

If I'm to have any chance, it's here. among all the people. the rush hour people walking in high heels and noisy men's dress shoes. From the first moment I walk through the doors, all sweating, I'm looking. seeing every face. some are blurry. some so fast like carnival lights. but none like hers. none that are just right. so I keep looking.

looking at every face, every back of the head that's at my level. who's sitting down in tucked away little corners or benches or shops or restaurants. My stomach jumps every time I see a glimpse of hair that's the exact color of hers. every time I see a mouth or a nose that could be hers.

I can feel her. feel her right here. inside my ribs, that's where I feel her. know she's been here and that she might, please, might still be here. But the place is so HUGE. so many twists and turns. so many places for us to miss each other, me going one way while she goes the next. but I feel her. it's burning. burning like a star in my chest and that's how bad I feel her.

The times I can breathe, I call her name. calling and calling. stopping everyone who passes me. holding them until I can see into their eyes. –*Elizabeth?*– I ask them. doesn't matter. boy or girl. anyone. I have to ask. just in case. in case the name means something to them. in case she's in disguise. in case of, I don't know. in case of anything. because I can't stop myself.

Oh, no. no, no, no. NO. NO fucking NO!

It's been too long, I know. it's been too many people passing me. too many. I'm back in the main room again. the big hallway. back right where I started. I'm standing at the ticket counter. the first in a wall lined with windows and people all standing in line, but I don't care about that. don't care about the rules that I'm supposed to follow because I'm pushing the man out of the way.

Asking the teller. *–Elizabeth?–*

He shrugs his shoulders. his eyes say I'm crazy. tell him that I am.

Pushing toward the next one. ask him. *–Elizabeth?–*

–Nope– he says.

The next one asking me if I'm okay. *–Are you lost, kid?–* but it's not me that's lost. Don't you get it? Don't any of you get it?

The next one. screaming. *–ELIZABETH?–*

Not here. and I'm falling apart. bent over at the waist because the pain is so big in my stomach.

And the next one. and the next.

Next one after that. crying. *–Elizabeth? please? PLEASE?–*

–Look, sorry, but you'll have to move.– because I'm a dis-turbance now. because the lines have stopped moving the way they're supposed to because I've cut to the front of all of them and now they are all looking at me. all the employ-ees. all the commuters.

The man at the booth is on his telephone, reporting me. at any second there'll be cops swarming down all over me. like insects. buzzing around me everywhere but I'm not hurting anybody. It's me. I'm the one in pain. I'm the one that's dying. NOT YOU! not any of you standing there. Sadness moving down my spine. moving so fast like a rocket. like a missile that's killing me.

But I get away. manage somehow to get my feet moving along the tiles to somewhere safe. somewhere hidden before the police get there to take me away. in white rooms with needles. in places you get permanently lost in. not me. leave me alone. EVERYONE JUST LEAVE ME ALONE! I have to be left alone. I am alone. that's how it needs to be. how I want it to be. for right now. for when I cry.

Over there. over by the restrooms away from everything. that's where I lean against the tile. slide down the wall. sink-ing. until I'm sitting. my knees up to my chest so I can hide

234

my head and let it out. let everything out. let myself give up. give into the pain in my throat that swallows my voice and I sob so quietly not a single person in the world will hear me.

I don't have any wings. They're bleeding. where they've been clipped. all gross and bloody. and I'm so sad because they used to be so pretty. hanging out there behind me so wide and transparent. fluttering. I miss them. I step on them. lying on the ground by my feet. I step on them.

I don't know how it happened. who did it. if it was me or someone really mean. But they're bleeding. all down my back. and I can see the scissors that did it. cut them off. It must've hurt, but it's funny because they don't hurt now. not when I'm standing here. wherever *here* is. I don't know exactly.

There's trees everywhere. really tall ones so that I can't see the sky because the trees grow so close together. so many branches touching the ones next to them like they're holding hands. with so many faces in their trunks. so many scary faces. I try not to look but that means I have to look at the wings that lie on the ground like they're fake. like they were never alive. all muddy where I stepped on them. stepped them into the ground.

I can't fly through the branches. they cover too much. and my wings have been cut off. the rusty scissors. and my pretty dress is all messy. not pretty anymore. torn up in places. decorated with stains. stains of my blood. of the muddy grass that is all around me. all wet. soggy. My feet are slipping. sinking into the ground.

I don't know which way to go. if I should start walking away or not. I don't want to stand here anymore. afraid I'll sink all the way under the ground. Don't want to look at the wings all mangled. they only remind me of how pretty I used to be. Besides, I'm all bloody. I should go somewhere. I'll probably die.

The shadows are getting closer. fly down on me like birds. But I still won't move. my ankles deep in the soil. And when I try to lift them, they only get stuck more. So I decide to just stand there. I will let them come down on me. eat me. swallow me up bite by bite because I'm bleeding anyway and I don't want to live without pretty wings. don't want to live if I can't fly ever again.

They're so close now. closer. I've closed my eyes. I can feel them right there. holding on to the air right in front of me, but not for long. I can feel them crawling on me. through the holes in my ugly dress. over my arms. between my fingers and they are cold and they're wet. covering me all the way and I hope. hope really hard. hope they can turn me into a shadow like them.

It's later now. Must be much later because the people have all disappeared onto trains and taken off to somewhere. just a few of them here and there. waiting for their turn. for their chance to leave too. Then the whole place will be empty.

The pain hasn't gone away none. Quieted down maybe, but hasn't gone away. It's still there. It's never been so bad. the pain. It wasn't this bad at home. I thought it would never get worse than that. if I left. that it would always not be so bad, because at least I wasn't there. But home was never like this. never like my ribs have been torn open and there's nothing inside. empty and damp. never like that.

I miss her. here. miss her so that my heart itches and scratches the inside of my throat. like I've swallowed chalk. and that's how it hurts when I think about the first time I held her hands. they were so cold. I'm not sure they ever warmed up. and now, knowing that there is nothing of her touch left. ever. and there is not enough of me to be mad. not enough of me to think of her dancing in the sun somewhere. playing. always happy. breaking my heart. always.

I can only see her when I close my eyes tight. see snapshots of her. bits and things I remember. It's too hard to try to remember any more than that. to picture the way she used to dance to keep warm. the way she would blow on her hands. or how she'd sing when she was in the shower and didn't know I could hear her. All of that I will try to forget because it hurts too much to remember. it will hurt less. forgetting will.

I start right away. going through all the things I want to forget about her. I want to forget the time I saw her playing with the Spanish children. the way she looked then. I will forget that. I want to forget her eyes. clean and blue. The time I looked into those eyes on the nights when we could hear Eric and Lily fighting in the next room. I want to forget that. I promise myself to forget that. I think I will forget that first. just like that. there. forgotten already.

I want to forget the way she snores. those little tiny snores that used to help me fall asleep. I want to forget the way she moved her hands to her face. the way she rubbed her eyes when she was tired. I want to forget all of that. every last bit of it because it only makes me miss her more to remember.

I think most of all I want to forget the time we kissed. I want to so bad, but I can't. the way the water felt on my skin. the light all around us on the shore. her face. her eyes when I leaned into her. I want to. Please let me forget that. please. I promise to remember everything else if I can forget that. pretend it never happened. Because it hurts too much that I'll have to keep that with me for the rest of my life.

If I could only see her the way she looked this morning. stretched across the sheets with her arms folded up behind her head. If I could only keep that like a photograph in my pocket forever. If I had a choice, that's how I'd choose to remember her. where I can't quite make out her face through the shadows. where her eyes are closed. asleep and perfect.

I cry again when I hear myself promising her that I would take care of her forever. *–Really?–* she said.

Remembering the way she said it is the most horrible thing, because I know now that I failed. Everyone was right when they told me I wouldn't be able to take care of her. they were right when they didn't want to let her stay. I should have let Ty throw her out, then I never would have been able to let her down.

I did.

–*I'm sorry, Elizabeth.*–

I see them staring at me. the telephones. I see them lined up along the wall across from me like they're something that I want or need. But I don't need them. There's no one I wish to speak to. no one who could make me feel better. no one except someone. except maybe him. I've meant to so many times but I haven't. couldn't. not until now. until there was no one else. no one. no one in the whole stupid world.

The dial tone scares me. listening to it humming into space. listening until it's beeping so fast because it needs me to feed numbers into it if I want to keep on holding it to my ear. I don't have any quarters. don't have anything left in me that will let me hang up the phone either.

There've been so many. so many people who have broken my heart. I don't want them to do it ever again. don't want anyone to. I want them all to make it up to me. I want to start with the first one. the first time I felt it. I want to start with him. with my daddy. HE OWES IT TO ME. he owes it to me to make everything okay. he owes me that much.

The operator is waiting for me to say something. waiting just a little longer before she'll be ready to hang up. Please don't. If you do, I know I will never pick up this phone again and I'm scared of that. scared not to say hello. My hands are shaking. I can't hold the hair out of my face any longer. I let it fall. let it hide me. sniff up everything so that I'm able to say the numbers. –*Collect please.*–

It's ringing. Maybe it's not him that will answer. Maybe it isn't his number anymore. Maybe I should hang up right now.

I can't hear anyone. I've been switched over. Then the woman's voice, the operator's voice comes back on. –*Your name?*–

Did someone answer? I didn't hear it. Is it him? did he answer? The operator asks me again. I'm breathing but I don't say anything. She asks me another time. *–Chan. um, Gretchen.–* and then the line clicks over again.

My heart stops beating. When the phone is silent, I won't let it beat. hold it in. so frightened that whoever it is who answered the phone will not accept the call. even more terrified that they might. that I will actually have to talk to him. I won't know what to say. I won't say anything. I could hang up right now. I should. But I have nothing else to try. nowhere else to go even if I wanted to. I can't start all over. can't start three years of my life all over. I can't. I'm not that brave. I'm not that . . . but the line has clicked over again.

It's the operator again and I almost faint. *–Okay, Gretchen, go ahead. And thank you for using AT&T.–*

–Gretchen? Gretchen?– the voice sounds more scared than mine. It's his voice. it's my dad. my dad. it's him. he's there. he's on the line. right there like he's right there beside me. his voice. I missed his voice so much. *–Sweetie? Are you there? Please let it be you! God, let it really be you!–*

I'm almost crying. It's worse than crying, really. It's something that makes it so I can't breathe. I can't speak. And he's saying my name over and over again. I can hear the tears in his voice. I can hear how sad he is. how hopeful. I want to say something. anything. I'm so afraid he'll hang up because I still haven't said a word. haven't even made a sound because it's that feeling. holding everything in. But then it loosens. just a little. enough for me to whisper

–daddy.–

and then it breaks. whatever it was holding me together, breaks. I'm sobbing into the phone. covering my mouth. I drop the phone because I have to cover my mouth with both hands so I can breathe. I can still hear his voice. but it's not right there anymore. It sounds far away. trapped in the phone swinging back and forth at the end of the cord. He's yelling my name. He's so happy. I can hear him.

It's like the hardest thing I've done when I pick up the phone again. *–Daddy?–* I say again even though I know he can't understand me. Everything's so muffled. talking between my fingers. choking it all back in. trying really hard.

–Gretchen?– he waits until he knows I'm listening. I know he wants me to. know he has something he wants to say to me. it's in his voice. something small. but I can hear it. even through the phone I can hear it.

–Gretchen? I looked for you. Did you hear me?– all the calmness in his voice is disappearing. I can hear him. trying to be strong. to be my dad. I can hear him trying so hard but he's crying now too.

–I looked, honey. I swear. to God, I swear I looked for you. I looked everywhere, Gretchen. I kept looking. but. but I never found you. and I thought . . . I just didn't know where to look anymore. but I never gave up, honey. I never–

I have to leave the lines blank here.

I have to. I don't have any words to say. I can hear how much pain he's in. how much he's been in for years. I can feel it. I'm so sorry. I'm sorry, daddy. sorry I ran away. sorry for what I did to you. How am I supposed to say that? What words am I supposed to say for that? I have to leave the spaces blank. Because I don't say anything. Because he doesn't say anything.

He's still crying. I know that. I've never stopped. He starts talking again. *–Gretchen. She's moved out, honey. She's gone.–* he's apologizing for everything. he can't stop. He's blaming himself and I'm so sad because I never meant to make him so sad. I'm so sad because he says it so many times. *–I'm sorry. I'm so sorry.–*

And I don't care. I just want him. want him to be there right now. I don't want to have to wait because I might not make it. I don't care about anything else but that.

–Daddy? I love you, Daddy.– and I can almost see him smiling. I have to drop the phone again. have to because I'm choking again and I need to cover my mouth. I'm spitting up tears so fast. so fast. there can't be many left. not anymore. there's been too many.

–Where are you? Do you want to come home, honey? Come home. Please. please, come home.–

and I do. I really do. I want to go home. more than anything in the whole world, I want to. I'm nodding my head because I can't say it. But I know he can see me. inside of him he can see me and he knows I want to. because he's my dad. he will always be my dad. will always know what I need.

He keeps talking because he's afraid to let me go. afraid he will never hear my voice again if he lets me get off the phone. he doesn't have to, though. I don't want to hang up.

just want to listen to his voice all night. listen to him talk, telling me how he thought he'd lost me forever. He's so happy. so scared. I tell him where I am and he doesn't ask me any questions. I'm so happy he doesn't because I've finally stopped crying enough to breathe and if he asks me anything I know I will start again.

He talks for hours. Just so that I can hear the sound of his voice. so that I can hug the phone close to me and pretend. He's coming. He's coming himself. Here. He's going to get on the first train in the morning. It leaves in a few hours. He'll be here three hours after that. He says he will stay on the phone with me until he has to leave. He's so afraid I won't be here when he gets here. He doesn't say so, but I know he is. That's why I promise. Why I say it even. Tell him –*I promise.*– a promise I know I can keep.

I tell him I'll wait by the information booth in the big hall. I won't move an inch until I see him, but that once I do, I'm going to run right up to him and he'll have to pick me up or else I will start crying again. I know I will be crying anyway.

–*Okay, sweetie, it's time. I have to go.*– It's early in the morning now. The night is gone. gone with so many words I could never count them. I don't say anything. I won't say goodbye because it's not goodbye. *–Don't move until I get there, okay? I'll be there so fast you won't even know it. I promise. Just. just stay there, okay?–*

–Okay.– then he says he loves me. for the first time in years and it feels so good to hear him say that. to hear those words for me from his voice. *–I love you too, daddy.–* but the last two words don't come out. I just couldn't get them out before it started up again. so I don't try. I just listen. waiting for the phone to hang up so that I can start counting the 10,000 and 800 seconds until I will see him walking up the stairs so I can hug him and not let go.

The tone is dead. buzzing. buzzing. But I keep it to my ear. keep my mouth against it. keep thinking if only I never left. wondering how I ever let it get to this point. how I ended up here. what little choices did I make that led to other ones that led me here. wondering how I could have done it all different. how I could've worked it out better. so that Elizabeth would be standing next to me while I was holding the phone. so that she would be coming with me.

It isn't how I imagined it. how I thought it was all going to turn out. But it never is, you know? And I can't blame myself for that. I won't let myself. I hope she doesn't blame me. that she will get away. do all the things we talked about because if I can't be there with her, I at least want to dream about it. dream she's okay. that she's okay forever.

I wanted more. I wanted something else. More than I guess I could ever have.

–*Excuse me. You done with that?*– I hadn't noticed. all the people. hadn't noticed them come in. that it was that time again. that there were people waiting for me to finish.

–*Um. Yeah. I'm done.*– and I put the phone back in its place. and I walk away. disappearing into the crowd. walking toward the information booth where I'll wait. wait for today to begin. wait for it to be the greatest day of all because I'm happy right now. happier than I've ever been.

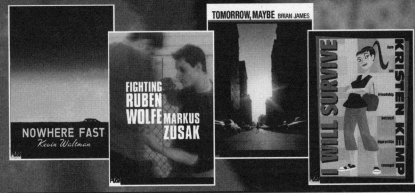